"Who could save the shuttle?" the Master asked

"Track?" Hudson answered, his voice low.

"Precisely, Colonel. Track will heroically attempt to defuse the bomb-rigged satellite in the shuttle's cargo bay. He will be unable to do so. When the bomb detonates, the biggest catastrophe in man's history in space will occur. And we will have eliminated Major Track, as well."

"I have to hand it to you, sir, that's—"

The Master of D.E.A.T.H. stopped at the bottom of the laboratory steps. He turned to Hudson, smiled, and said, "Diabolical?"

**Now available in the exciting new series
from Gold Eagle Books**

TRACK

by Jerry Ahern

TRACK

Revenge of the Master

JERRY AHERN

A GOLD EAGLE BOOK FROM
WORLDWIDE

TORONTO · NEW YORK · LONDON · PARIS
AMSTERDAM · STOCKHOLM · HAMBURG
ATHENS · MILAN · TOKYO · SYDNEY

Another one for my old buddy Jerry Buergel,
who has done many crazy things
with the Aherns over the years.
All the best to you,
Judy, Jerry and Lisa.

Special acknowledgment
to my pal Sid Woodcock
for invaluable technical assistance.

First edition August 1985

ISBN 0-373-62008-X

1

Don Carlo Capezi found himself doing this more and more, shuffling through memories. From the center drawer of his desk he took a photograph of his daughter, a school teacher who had been kidnapped, raped and murdered by terrorists. She had been a pretty girl, but he couldn't cry for her anymore, only for himself for missing her. Under the photograph he found the note from Major Dan Track, the man who had tried to save his daughter and earned his undying gratitude.

He unfolded the note and read it again. The sunlight streaming through the window was warm and pleasant on his face and hands.

Dear Don Carlo,

I just wanted to write to let you know how deeply I appreciated your help in the recent situation in Mexico. And how deeply I lament the loss of three of your men in the process. They were brave men. Without them it would have been impossible to stop Hummingbird, who of course revealed herself as Potempkin.

Without them, it would have been a certainty that many more lives would have been lost. Emilio, the pilot who works for your Mexican associates, was a brave and loyal ally, as well. I was happy to hear that his injuries were minor and he has recovered fully. I also heard that Rudy was on the mend—he was a good man to fight beside.

You have spoken of being in my debt for my efforts on behalf of your late daughter, but I am the one truly in your debt. If there is anything I can ever do to assist you, within the limits that we both know govern our relationship, I would feel dishonored were you not to call upon me.

It is in this spirit of friendship that I write to warn you of something that may concern you. When we were able to end the career of the mercenary Col. Thomas Beal, we also incurred the wrath of an organization known as D.E.A.T.H. By association with us, you, too, may have earned its enmity.

To a man of your position, this is a ridiculous warning, but you should be careful. If any information concerning the Directorate or the Master of D.E.A.T.H. comes to my attention, I'll be sure to pass it along.

Desiree Goth and I are enjoying a much-needed rest. My nephew George is with his father at my house in New Mexico. For now, all is well.

Sincerely,
Dan Track

Carlo Capezi folded the letter in half and placed it back in the drawer. He respected Dan Track, despite the fact that Track was a man of the law and he, in frankness to himself, was not.

There was a knock at the door of his office, and as he looked up the door opened and his personal bodyguard, Eduardo, smiled and said, "Forgive me, Don Carlo, but Rudy has returned to work today and wished to pay his respects."

"Excellent. Please send him in."

Eduardo stepped back from the door and Rudy's face appeared. Closing the door behind him, he approached the desk.

"Rudy! You seem well—do you feel well, my friend?" Carlo Capezi began

"Yes, Don Carlo. The burns are almost healed. And only my left leg is still a little stiff. They were clean breaks, the doctors said."

"Your family is well? There is nothing they need?"

"Yes, Don Carlo, they are well. It is one reason why I felt I must come to you and offer my thanks. While I was in the hospital, my wife and my son wanted for nothing. I am forever in your debt for your kindness to my family, Don Carlo, and I seek to find some way by which to show my gratitude."

Don Carlo stood up, studying Rudy's face. The dark hair always looked as though it was uncombed, giving him the appearance of a renegade. Rudy had a slight build, but was very tall. There were a few bright pink spots on Rudy's otherwise olive cheeks and chin, reminders of the burns he had received when the beach house in Mexico had been attacked.

"And tell me, your father's pistol was not lost to you?"

"No, Don Carlo, I still have the Bolo Mauser." Rudy smiled, patting the left side of his coat.

"You speak of finding some way to express your gratitude, but you have done this by coming to me in friendship. Your loyalty ever since you were a boy, your fine service have demonstrated your gratitude. And should you find yourself in need, or should there be trouble and your family need anything, your gratitude can best be shown by remembering that I am here to call upon. I have found a nice house of prostitution that is in a fine area and is very clean. Little trouble exists there, and until your health is fully restored I want you to serve me there to guard the interests of our family. The hours are flexible—" he allowed himself a conspiratorial smile "—and should you feel weak during your recuperation, there is always a bed you can lie down on."

"Thank you, Don Carlo. The doctor says I

should be completely recovered in another six weeks."

"Excellent. When you have, come and speak with me again and we'll find other duties more befitting your talents."

"Thank you, Don Carlo—for my family and for myself."

Don Carlo extended his hand, and with a bit of hesitation, Rudy grasped it warmly.

Don Carlo clapped his hand on Rudy's shoulder. "You're a good boy, Rudy. Go talk to the rest of the boys and renew old friendships. Eduardo will be driving me into Miami for the luncheon these Children's Hunger people have insisted on having in my honor. After that, Eduardo can drive you to your new place of work and introduce you to the madam there. Then take the rest of the week to be with your family. You can start Saturday night."

"Yes, thank you, Don Carlo." Rudy bowed slightly. Don Carlo smiled and released his trusted man's hand. Rudy went to the door, opened it and disappeared into the reception area. Eduardo poked his head through the doorway, after rapping on it once.

"Yes?"

"It's time for us to leave for the luncheon, Don Carlo."

"Luncheons—this is silliness. All because I write a big check to feed starving children. What

man would not do such a thing? Very well." He
started across his office and toward the door.. . .

THERE WAS ONE GUY Rudy particularly wanted to
see—young Gino Lambesi, and Gino was on the
roof of the house. It took Rudy some time to
climb the stairs leading to the roof, but he managed it well enough. He laughed at himself; after
what happened in Acapulco when the Commun-
ists attacked the beach house, he was very cautious
about rooftops. But that would go away, he knew.
As one of the don's closest security people, he frequently found himself on the roof of the house.

As he reached the top of the stairs, he could see
Gino sitting on the edge of the roof where it rose
about twelve inches to form a lip. Beside Gino was
an M-16 propped against the eaves.

Rudy walked across the roof, shouting, "Hey,
Gino!"

"Rudy!" Gino Lambesi got up and ran across
the rooftop and the two men embraced, Rudy
slapping the younger man on the back. "Rudy,
how are you?"

Rudy laughed and said, "Hell, I'm fine. Sore
like the devil, and the burns itch but I don't have
to shave in the mornings, so it's a mixed bag.
How's the new little girl?"

"Hey—seven and a half pounds. And I was
there when my wife had her. Scared the shit outta
me, but I watched it all the time, anyway."

"You get back to your post before the don sees you—he was going to his car."

"Right." They walked together toward the edge of the roof, Gino lighting a cigarette, then offering one to Rudy.

"Ever since I got burned, I lost the taste for it, you know," Rudy said.

They were at the edge of the roof now, and easing out his left leg, Rudy sat on the lip of concrete. Gino picked up his M-16 and cradled it in the crook of his right arm like a hunter would hold a shotgun. "Man, we were worried about you," Gino began. "Too bad about Bob and the other guys."

Rudy shrugged and said, "This Dan Track, the guy the don speaks so highly of, he's a good man. Him and his friends nailed all those Commie bastards."

Gino didn't say anything, and Rudy looked over the edge of the roof and saw Carlo Capezi leave the building. The old don looked up as he always did and shot them a wave. Rudy waved back, glancing at Gino who was doing the same.

"A finer gentleman you wouldn't wanna meet," Gino said, nodding in the direction of Capezi.

"That's no lie. The don took good care of my family—"

"Yeah. You know he was griping about going to this charity luncheon, but I think he's looking forward to it. They're giving him some kinda plaque.''

Rudy nodded, still listening, but watching the don as he entered the Cadillac.

"I think he's feeling good," Gino continued. "Been a long time since he felt good—he's smiling again.''

"Losing the girl hit him hard.''

Rudy stopped talking, watching as Eduardo walked around the car and climbed behind the wheel.

He could hear the Cadillac's engine, sounding rough. Later he remembered that he had started to say, "I think Eduardo should get that looked at—''

Then the fireball belched skyward, and the noise of the explosion deafened him as an invisible fist hammered him off the lip of concrete and onto the surface of the roof.

His face slammed hard into the hot cinders. He rolled onto his back and raised himself up on his elbows. Gino was on the roof just a yard from him, a piece of chrome off the Cadillac sticking through his forehead, his open black eyes staring up into the sun, blood trickling over his nose.

Rudy couldn't stand—his left leg screamed at him. Painfully, he crawled toward the lip of concrete, the Bolo Mauser in his fist. If it was some kind of attack—

He looked over the edge.

"Jesus! Jesus!" he said silently.

There was nothing left of the Cadillac except a smoldering, twisted frame and two lumps—one in the front seat where the wheel had been, the other in the back on the passenger side. "Jesus!" Rudy repeated. He crossed himself and prayed for the soul of Carlo Capezi.

2

He hadn't ridden an elephant for many years—and he hardly found the feeling refreshing. The elephant had a particularly lumpy backbone, and the conjunction of his own posterior with the elephant was proving entirely uncomfortable. He had contacted Desiree first and she had agreed with his judgment that Abdul Kefari was a valued old customer and if he required that a shipment be delivered under Zulu's personally watchful eye then it should be so. The overseas flights had taken a long time and proved tedious, but they were a holiday compared to the two-day ride by Land Rover accompanying the cargo trucks, and then the shifting of the arms and the related gear to the backs of pack elephants and the trek through the jungle.

It was in its second day now and Zulu consoled himself with visions of the hot bath he could soak in when he returned to Singapore, where civilization had its pleasures.

The elephant suddenly made a violent noise like a sneeze, and Zulu's body rocked with the vibrations that worked their way through the massive beast's body.

He resettled himself at the floppy-eared pachyderm's nape and shifted the full flap holster at his belt that held the Browning Hi-Power. He moved the holster slightly forward. The elephant started up a rise, and Zulu shifted his weight forward, knotting his fists on the animal's ears.

Ahead, beyond the walkers who broke the trail with their machetes, someone was shouting in Chinese. Chinese was not one of his languages. Zulu twisted on the elephant's back and called behind him, "Shin? What's going on up ahead?"

"One of the boys says he's seen something strange."

"Does he say what it is?" Zulu asked the almost painfully thin Chinese.

"He didn't."

"We'd better take a look."

Zulu looked over the sloping cranium of the elephant and beyond, hearing as Shin shouted something to the men ahead of him.

He drew up on the chain that led to the elephant's right front foot and the animal stopped.

He rapped his mahout stick against the beast's left front leg and the elephant raised the leg, bent at the knee. Zulu swung his right leg over the animal's head, put his foot on the elephant's knee and hopped to the ground.

Sweat poured from every pore of his body, and

his khaki bush shirt was plastered to him as he walked up the small rise. His back ached from the elephant ride.

Shin was shouting from behind him. "Mr. Zulu! Do not—"

Zulu lost the rest of the words as he heard a bolt click. A submachine gun. Zulu broke into a run, at a right angle to the path and toward a spot where the ground dropped off. He threw himself forward as the gunfire began, and the screams of men and elephants filled the air, almost drowning out the incessant light chatter of submachine guns and the heavier burps of assault-rifle fire.

He was airborne, crashing through a huge frond of bright green, then slamming into the dirt and the rocks and rolling. He grabbed the flap of his holster, tugging it open, finding the butt of the Hi-Power.

Skidding into the base of a large tree covered with hanging vines, he rolled back, winded.

Gunfire and shouts continued to come from the path above.

Zulu slapped his battered fedora to his head, and in one fluid motion his left hand was on the slide of the Hi-Power, jacking it back.

A sudden rustling alerted him to someone moving through the brush above him. As Zulu raised the Hi-Power to fire he heard a familiar voice shout, "Wait, sir!"

Shin came crashing through the foliage, Zulu's

870 riot pump and gray engineer's bag loaded with shells in his left hand, a revolver in his right. His footing went, and the lanky twenty-five-year-old Chinese skidded down the steep slope. Zulu upped the safety on the Hi-Power just in time to break Shin's slide with his arms and stagger back with him against the tree trunk.

More gunfire creased the air.

"Who are they, Shin?"

Shin shrugged. "We had no reports of terrorists working this region."

More gunfire exploded, and the leaves near Zulu's left arm shredded. Zulu shoved the Chinese to the ground, throwing himself flat next to the man. "How's it look up there?" he asked Shin.

Shin looked Zulu in the eyes and said, "All our men are dead."

Men started to shout above them. Zulu looked inquiringly at Shin, and Shin said, "I don't know. It sounds like Vietnamese."

"Merde," Zulu muttered. He snatched the riot shotgun and bag of shells from Shin. "We'll run for it—come on!"

Zulu pushed himself up, working the pump, pulling the trigger with the shotgun's muzzle aimed up the hillside. He tromboned the action again and ran. "Come on!"

There was only one chance—they must reach the site where Abdul Kefari was to have met them.

That would mean either death, if Kefari was in league with the attackers, or sanctuary.

It was a trap, and as he ran Zulu cursed himself. He should have smelled it. And either Abdul was the willing bait or an unwilling dupe. Zulu's dealings with the man over the years made him think—hope—it was the latter.

He kept running, Shin panting beside him.

3

He had met her in the supermarket. A dust storm was brewing outside and they were both in a hurry to get their shopping done before the storm broke. Their carts had collided between two cat-food displays that made the aisle impossibly narrow. They had knocked over both displays and sent a few hundred small tins of Kitty Kitchen rolling across the floor.

After doing the "My fault; No, my fault" dance, they both started to laugh and tried to put the display back in some kind of order. Soon a clerk arrived, shaking his head and wondering aloud how some people managed to tie their shoes in the morning. George and the woman had looked at each other, shrugged, and started off down the aisle together.

George had never bought so many things—just to slow down their progress.

When she'd asked what he did to pay for all those groceries, he had told her he was a sort of private policeman. "A security guard?" Not that. "A detective?" Sort of. He told her he specialized in counterterrorist activities for a group known as the Consortium.

She said, "Hmm," as if counterterrorists were encyclopedia salesmen and turned toward the checkout counter. As an afterthought she added, "By the way, my name's Ellen. Ellen Mansfield."

"I'm George Beegh," he had replied.

The dust storm was raging by the time they left the supermarket and he had helped her get her groceries into her Volkswagen Beetle. Then she had driven him over to where his Bronco was parked and helped him pack his bags away.

The dust storm was howling in a thick yellow rage, and it was cold. She told him he'd never get into the mountains in one piece and invited him to follow her home and wait out the storm over some coffee.

She had a small flat in a modern apartment village that looked as though it belonged in the English countryside, at least from the outside.

He had helped her inside with her groceries, and George Wilson Beegh had found himself talking to her, telling her about his mother's ordeal in Russia and his father's rescue from a Soviet prison. After hearing his tale she stared at him incredulously and he told her that he was one of the group the press had labeled the Vindicators.

She looked at him in silence, sizing him up, trying to gauge whether he was just another kook. "Well," she said, lifting her shoulders, "I'll try not to step on your cape."

They had both laughed over that.

The dust storm wound down as they talked, but he stayed for dinner. Afterward, they had a drink and talked some more. When he left, about nine in the evening, Ellen had kissed him quickly on the cheek, then shut the door.

At eleven that night he woke her up when he called her on the telephone.

They had seen each other every day since.

His father had been called away for another of the seemingly interminable series of CIA debriefings, and alone in Track's house, except for the cat, Dorothy, he had called Ellen and asked her to drive up, offering to fix dinner.

He alternated his time between shooing Dorothy off his lap and reading the book on perennials that Ellen had given him. She was a botanist and, from what he had learned about her when he had picked her up at work, she was a very good one and the youngest female assistant director of a facility of equal size anywhere in the country.

He knew nothing about plants except watering the fig tree and the jade plant that his uncle kept at his house. Tassels LaTour had shown him how. Tassels, his uncle's occasional secretary, had always liked plants and now had an entire garden

full of them in the spring—or at least she said she
did. But he couldn't ask Tassels LaTour to help
decipher passages of the book that were Greek to
him, because Tassels was away visiting her grand-
niece in San Francisco.

So he skipped that paragraph and went on to
the next as Dorothy climbed on his lap again.

A while later, he heard the car in the driveway. When he opened the door Ellen was already
standing on the step, a bag of groceries in each
arm.

"I remembered what you were buying that first
time we met, so I thought I'd better bring some
things of my own along just in case."

He stood there, looking at her. Her dark brown
hair fell in waves past her shoulders, and her large
brown eyes were staring up at him. She was wearing a heavy white sweater over a blue plaid blouse,
a light blue A-line skirt and dark blue low-heeled
shoes. The only jewelry she wore was a pair of
very tiny gold pierced earrings and the thin gold
chain he had given her for her twenty-fifth birth-
day a week ago.

"Are you going to take the groceries, George?"
she asked.

"Sure." George smiled, taking the bags from
her arms. As he did, she leaned up and planted a
kiss on his mouth, then walked quickly past him.
Dorothy was running up to Ellen, rolling over on
the floor at her feet, and Ellen started scratching

the cat's belly. "She likes you," George said. "So do I."

"She just likes the way I scratch her," Ellen said with a laugh. "Don't you, Dorothy, baby?"

George just watched her play with Dorothy. Ellen started to speak again. "I brought a special treat for you, too, Dorothy—how's about some nice fresh tuna fish, huh?"

It was as if Dorothy understood, because the cat rolled over, was to her feet in a split second and bounded across the living room and jumped to the kitchen counter beyond, meowing so loudly she sounded almost obscene, George thought.

"I was glad you could come," George said.

"I was glad you asked me, George," he heard her say. He set down the groceries, starting to empty the bags as he looked across the counter and into the living room. Ellen was tying a blue denim bib-front apron into place as she left the chair and the fireplace. "I always come prepared."

George laughed and started to unpack the grocery bags, taking out containers of spices, a bag of flour and an odd-looking machine. "What do you do with this?"

"You make spaghetti with it."

"You actually make spaghetti—don't just take it out of a package?"

"Lots of times I take it out of a package, but sometimes I make it. I figured I'd make some tonight. You like spaghetti, right? Everybody likes spaghetti."

"I love spaghetti," George told her. "I think I love you, too."

She just looked at him, standing there on the other side of the counter.

George cleared his throat. "How about a drink?"

"Look in the other bag."

He obeyed and produced a three-liter bottle of burgundy.

"Goes with the spaghetti," she told him.

He didn't watch her eyes as he fished down two tumblers and then uncorked the wine bottle. "I said, I love you."

"You said you think you love me."

"I've decided—I love you."

"I love you, too, George," she replied, her eyes smiling as he looked up from the wine and passed a glass across the counter to her.

"What are we gonna do about it?"

"What are you thinking of doing?"

"I don't know—got any ideas?"

"A woman always has ideas. Go play with Dorothy or finish reading that book I gave you. If I don't get this spaghetti started, we'll never eat."

And she started around the counter and George took her into his arms. "The spaghetti..." she began.

"Can wait," George told her, drawing her closer to him. She turned her head up to look at him and he touched his lips to hers, lightly, then very hard as he folded his arms closer around her.

She was kissing him back, and he felt her hands touch his face, and then her hands moved to his chest and she was pushing against him. He let her go. "You want me to go to bed with you now." It was a statement, not a question.

"Take this the way I mean it," George replied. "I wanted you to go to bed with me the first time I saw you."

"I know. But I won't—"

George licked his lips. His cigarettes were back by the chair and he suddenly wanted one badly.

"What do you want from me?" he asked.

"Maybe too much—I don't know."

George cleared his throat. "Will you marry me?"

She looked at him hard. "Just to go to bed with you?" she teased. "Yes. Yes, I think I will."

He took her into his arms again and kissed her mouth lightly. She smiled and whispered, "I love you, George," and she put her head against his chest.

THEY SAT BESIDE THE FIREPLACE. Dinner was over, and they each had a glass of red wine. Ellen's legs were curled up under her skirt.

"You sure you want to marry me?" she asked.

"Yeah, I'm sure. Trust the judgment of an experienced man, already."

"Okay."

George lit a cigarette.

"That's bad for your health."

"You can reform me after we're married," he told her.

"Okay."

"When do you want to do it?"

"When do you want to?"

"Why don't we do it pretty quick. Maybe, get a license tomorrow?"

"At lunch?"

"At lunch is okay," George agreed.

"How do you feel about children?"

"Can't stand the little suckers, but I suppose we can have some. They'll grow on me."

"I'd like that."

George wrapped his arms around her and drew her close as he snapped the cigarette butt into the hearth. He kissed her very lightly on the forehead and watched how the firelight made her skin look so warm.

Then, just for a second, he felt a chill, like something was wrong. Had he heard a sound outside the house? His blood ran cold, and he looked at the mantel where the Colt Combat Government lay. Then he heard the shots and pushed Ellen to the floor. He sprang up, reaching for the gun.

With the suddenness of a clap of thunder, subgunfire ripped across the wall near the mantel-piece. Glass shattered and Ellen screamed. George's fingers closed over the butt of the Colt, his body swinging around, his left hand jacking back the slide. The .45 bucked in his right fist toward the windows that flanked the front door. A man with a submachine gun rocked back, slamming hard against the doorframe, the subgun firing into the ceiling.

George took a step forward, and a chunk of wall blew out where his head had just been. He wheeled around, feeling the hot sickness and then the cold in his left forearm as he pumped the Colt's trigger again.

The second subgunner's face seemed to vaporize.

George fired twice again.

The gunman's body snapped back through the front window.

George reached to the mantelpiece for the spare magazine he kept there. He buttoned out the Colt magazine in his pistol and slammed the charged eight-rounder in place.

Everything was eerily quiet.

He looked down to the floor in front of the couch.

Ellen.

George dropped to his knees in the growing pool of blood around her and he began to cry as he cradled her head in his arms, the .45 still in his fist. She was breathing, but he couldn't help thinking she was dying. "Ellen?" The voice that called her name wasn't his own, he decided, because he was a grown man and this was a little boy's voice full of sobbing and very afraid.

4

"I've decided—Nice is nice."

"Do you want people to think you can't speak French?" Desiree said.

Dan Track shrugged and reached out to put a hand on her arm as they walked up the sweeping flight of stone steps leading to the front doors of Breechmore House. Track thought that Desiree, in her dress with the long narrow skirt, looked like a princess on her way to a ball.

He wondered how to classify himself. In his black tuxedo and butterfly bow tie he felt like a penguin who had fallen into a vat of starch.

"What are you thinking?" Desiree asked him when they reached the top of the steps.

"About formal wear, if you really want to know."

"You'll get used to it. You look very dashing, very handsome. The bow tie accentuates your jaw, and the cut of your jacket shows off your build."

"As long as it doesn't show off my gun," Track said as he smiled at her. Beneath the jacket of the tuxedo he wore an Alessi speed-break diagonal shoulder holster, and inside it was one of the relatively new and hard-to-come-by Detonics Pocket 9s. It paid to have friends.

They walked toward the stone facade of the country house and as Track started to reach for the door a doorman pulled it open. As Desiree stepped through, the music rushed out to meet them. He could hear faint laughter, and virtually smell the champagne flowing.

He didn't like parties, but Desiree had done something she rarely did—she'd insisted. The earl of Breechmore and his wife were among her oldest friends. Apparently Breechmore was once a smuggler himself until marriage had relieved him of the necessity to work, as Desiree had put it.

Track had acquiesced.

Track had bought the tuxedo.

Track now regretted it.

Liveried young men approached and took Desiree's wrap and Track's trench coat. As they started across the black-and-white tile floor of the foyer and toward the grand ballroom, Desiree said, "Do you see the women watching you?"

Track looked at her with surprise. "They're watching you," he said. "Because you make them look like Cinderella's sisters." And she did, Track thought—the brilliant white silk of the dress highlighted her rich tan and made her black hair somehow more lustrous, and her blue eyes somehow brighter. Around her neck she wore a single strand of diamonds, each stone flawless, shimmering, perfect—as she was. Her usual diamond-set watch was on her left wrist, and she wore nothing else except small diamond pierced earrings, which were only visible when she brushed her hair away from her face with the back of her hand.

Exquisite was the word for Desiree Goth, Track thought.

He fished in his jacket pocket and retrieved a printed invitation as they approached the entrance to the ballroom. A liveried man at the doorway accepted it with a smile, nodding curtly and saying, *"Merci, monsieur, madame."*

Track guided Desiree past the young man and into the grand room.

He didn't like the place—he could tell that already.

Too many people. Too much empty laughter. "Steady," Desiree whispered, hugging his arm, smiling.

Track mentally shrugged, then formed a smile on his face—he would try to like it, for her.

At least, he thought as they drifted into the crowd and Desiree smiled toward a few of the faces and seemed to consciously ignore some of the others, the music was satisfactory. The orchestra was playing the 1940s standard, "What's New?" Track curled his right arm around Desiree's waist, asking her, "Wanna dance, kid?"

"Do you dance?"

"Sure. Remember that first time we met?"

She smiled. "I could still ask the question—do you dance?"

"Being a poor dancer was part of my cover then," Track replied, smiling himself.

"I doubt it," Desiree told him, letting him take her into his arms, bending her body against him as he guided her onto the crowded dance floor.

Her head rested against his chest, her hand locked in his. "I don't like this place," Track said, "but I like the company."

"You'll have a good time. Algie's a lot of fun—really."

"Algie?"

"Sir Algernon Cole, the earl of Breechmore. His wife's a little on the stuffy side, but she'll probably like you. You're her type—tall, dark, handsome—and she loves mustaches. I'm certain that's why she married Algie—he has a mustache like a walrus at the zoo."

"I can hardly wait to meet them." Track said with a noticeable lack of enthusiasm.

He felt a tap on his shoulder, and instinct took over for a split second and he started to turn fast. He caught himself and raised his hand to brush back his hair instead of reaching for the pistol under his tuxedo. A very tall man, with laughing gray eyes and bald except for a fringe that circled his head like a wilted laurel wreath, stood beside him. And he had a very huge, very brushy mustache. Like a walrus.

"Algie," Track heard Desiree saying, and then suddenly Desiree was in the man's arms, kissing his cheek. The walrus held her close. "Algie," Desiree repeated, "this is Daniel Track."

Track extended his hand. "Sir Algernon—"

"Algie, please, Major."

Track's eyebrow rose, and the walrus smiled. "I do my homework on people. Old habits die hard."

"I'll call you Algie if you'll call me Dan."

"Agreed, old chap, agreed."

Breechmore's handclasp was firm, just a few degrees shy of a crusher, Track decided.

"My God, you look better each time I see you," Breechmore said to Desiree. "Dishonesty must agree with you." He laughed. Desiree bent her head against his chest, then tossed her head back, the diamond earrings showed for a split second. "I'm so glad you could come," Breechmore continued. "Almost everyone here is a friend of Prissy's and—"

Track looked beyond the hulking, gleaming-domed earl of Breechmore. She was tall, thin, her honey blond hair up, ringing curls escaping their confinement at the nape of her neck.

"Dan!" she exclaimed. "When I saw who Desiree was bringing with her—"

"Priscilla," Track whispered, and the woman

was in his arms, kissing him hard on the mouth, harder than she should have with her husband there, he thought, but not as hard as she had kissed him the last time.

"Oh—it's been so long," she said, smiling and slightly breathless as she stepped back from him, looking him up and down, her brown eyes warm and bright.

"Very long," Track told her.

"Hi, there." Desiree interjected, and suddenly Track started to laugh. "I gather you two know each other?"

Priscilla had her arms around his neck and was leaning against him. "Dan and I were old friends, before I met Algie."

"Major Track seems to be a man of many surprises," Breechmore said.

"It was Captain Track, then," Priscilla added, uncoiling her left arm from Track and putting it around her husband's neck. "And he was the horniest captain I ever met in any army. Our relationship was very intense."

There was an embarrassed silence. Track smiled at Desiree. He wished he'd worn his cowboy boots because he would have had a better chance of sinking into them than he had with the Florsheim loafers.

"Why don't we all have a drink in the library— get away from the music and the people and talk," Breechmore suggested.

"That's a wonderful idea." Priscilla smiled. "Dan, let's let Desiree and Algie go on ahead. I haven't danced with you in—"

"Years," Track supplied.

She half pushed him back among the dancers, his arms going around her as he whirled her away. "You trying to make trouble or what, Pris?" Track asked her, his voice low.

She kissed his neck, then leaned her head against his chest. He noted that she still used the same perfume, and her hair smelled of the same shampoo. And as she snuggled against him, he felt that her breasts had that fantastic heat they had always had.

"Would I try to get you in trouble, Dan?" she said, her voice full of mischief.

"Yes," Track told her, touching his lips to her forehead. "But it's good to see you. I'd heard you'd married somebody with a title."

"His title, my money," she said sharply. "It seemed like a good idea at the time."

"At the time—sure," Track said, looking past her, trying to spot Desiree and Pris's husband.

"Listen, they won't miss us. They can talk about the good old days in smuggling or something. Do you know how many bedrooms this house has?"

"No. But it fascinates me—I love older homes."

"Fifteen!"

"And I bet you've tried each and every one of them," Track replied, feeling at once that he was being unfair.

"What a thing to say to your old lover," she admonished.

Track shrugged. "You know me—honest to a fault."

"That's why we broke up, wasn't it, darling?"

Track didn't answer. Sometimes she wasn't bad in the honesty department, either, he thought.

"Are you and Desiree a thing?" Priscilla continued.

"Yes, we're a thing."

"Hmm. Desiree Angelique Goth—what a contrived name."

"Prettier name than Priscilla Langley Brookes Cole."

"Touché. We could get into bed just for old times' sake."

"I'm not that old. Besides, I talk better standing up."

"You never would do that—cheat on somebody—would you?"

"Never did on you," Track told her. The song had shifted away from the 1940s to the sixties and a downtempo version of the Beatles' song, "Michelle."

"Remember, we used to dance to this a lot," Priscilla said dreamily.

"We never danced to this a lot," Track replied, the soul of romance.

"Well, we would have if somebody had played it. We did most of our dancing under the sheets if I recall."

"You recall correctly," Track said with a smile. "You look terrific—either you could have nailed me for the European version of the Mann Act ten years ago or—"

"Or what? I'm remarkably well preserved?"

Track laughed. "Something like that, I guess."

"You look good, too. I'd love to see you with your clothes off."

"No, you wouldn't. I've wasted away to nothing," Track told her.

"Muscles—that's what I feel." Her hand was kneading his forearm.

"Just clever padding in the jacket."

"I'll bet. You just as good in bed?"

"You'll never know," Track replied as he grinned.

"Come on, tell me."

"Ask Desiree," Track told her, but then thought better of it. "On second thought, don't ask Desiree."

"Oh, yes, I will. Algie knows all about you. Every time he doesn't live up to expectations, I tell him about this American Army captain who used to screw my socks off in Germany."

"That's what I always liked about you—such a perfect lady."

"Well, you did screw my socks off. Remember that time you couldn't wait for me to get out of my panty hose and you—"

"Yes," Track said. "I remember. Memories recalled from years ago tend to be exaggerated."

"Bullshit. If Desiree's got you in her bed every night, she's the luckiest woman alive."

Track looked into her brown eyes. She pursed her lips into a kiss and blew it at him. "I mean that," she whispered.

Track didn't know what to say to her.

She leaned her head against his chest. "How about one more time?"

"I don't think so. It wouldn't be fair to Desiree or your husband."

"I mean it, Dan. You used to say I was fantastic."

"You were fantastic."

"I still am fantastic—try me."

"I'll just have to console myself with the memory of what I'm missing."

And then he felt her hand. It had dropped from his arm to his crotch. "Stop that," Track said, trying to keep dancing.

"I'll drive you crazy right here on the dance floor. You won't be able to walk away from me unless you brought a hat with you." She laughed.

Track knew she was right. "Knock it off," he said quickly.

"That's what I'm trying to do."

"You know what I mean," Track whispered, hardly able to dance anymore.

"What's Desiree going to say? Hmm?" She laughed.

"She'll shoot you with that little .38 of hers."

"Or maybe she'll shoot you."

Track's hand moved up her back, finding the zipper for the midnight blue dress she wore. The zipper ran halfway down her rear end, and he started moving the zipper slowly down her back. "What are you doing?" she said in sudden alarm.

"Taking your dress off."

"Not in the middle of the dance floor!"

"Why not?" Track said as he smiled.

"You wouldn't!"

Track worked the zipper down a few more inches. "Try me."

"You—"

Track looked down at her and grinned.

Her hand pulled away from his pants, and he pulled the zipper of her dress up.

He danced with her a moment longer, to let nature take its course, then started edging toward the far side of the dance floor where there was a set of high double doors that he hoped led to the library.

"You wouldn't have taken my dress off," she declared, but not quite sure of herself.

"You just keep thinking that," Track told her. "But I do think about you sometimes, and I bet you still are terrific."

He drew her beside him, and started walking off the dance floor. "The library?"

"The library," Priscilla answered, hugging his arm. "Dan?"

"Yeah?" He had both hands on the door handles as he looked at her.

"You weren't the only man I ever made love to—you know that."

"Yeah," he whispered, smiling at her.

"But you were the only man I ever loved. I realized that a couple of years too late."

Track leaned toward her. Taking her face in his hands, he kissed her lightly on the lips. He wanted to say, "I'm sorry," but he thought she might not understand how he meant it. So he just looked at her for a moment. "You like the old songs," he whispered. "Remember this one? 'It's the wrong time, and the wrong place—though your face is lovely it's the wrong face.' Remember that one?"

She leaned her head against his chest. "Uh-huh, I remember that one." He touched his lips to her hair and opened the library doors, stepping aside to let her pass inside. She looked at him a moment and smiled. Her eyes seemed brighter than they should have been, and they were teary. "I remember that one,'' she repeated, then walked past him toward the bar on the far side of the library.

Track followed her and surveyed the room. The ceiling was at least twenty feet high, and against two walls rich mahogany bookshelves soared from floor to ceiling. On the far wall a massive stone fireplace imposed itself on the room. He saw Desiree looking at him as she stood beside the mantel.

Track winked at her and nodded.

As the corners of her mouth turned up, her neutral expression changed into a smile. He walked across the room toward her, ignoring Breechmore who sat in a brocaded armchair on the opposite side of the fire. Track put his arm around Desiree and kissed her and then turned to his host, smiling. ''I was having withdrawal symptoms—forgive me.''

''Not at all, old chap. Desiree's just the sort of woman who could give any man withdrawal symptoms. It's the other sort of withdrawal symptoms I'm not fond of.'' He glanced over his shoulder toward his wife. Her back was turned to them, and Track heard glasses clinking. ''There is withdrawal in the psychological sense, and in the physical sense.''

Track made himself smile and raised both hands palms outward. He said nothing.

Breechmore spoke again. ''So you are the amorous American Army captain.''

"You have a nice flair for alliteration."

"So pleased you noticed."

Algie stood up. Behind him, Priscilla was approaching, two glasses balanced awkwardly in each hand. "Let's see if I got this right," she enthused, starting to laugh. "Desiree likes gin and tonic, Dan likes anything—but he especially likes a double shot of Seagrams Seven over ice with a splash."

"Right." Track smiled at her, suddenly feeling very bad that he hadn't been kinder just now on the dance floor and ten years ago, as well.

"And Algie, a vodka martini for you—"

Track interrupted her. "And two fingers of Cutty and an ice cube."

She looked at him and smiled. "It's usually four fingers of Cutty these days." She handed around the glasses.

Algie raised his martini glass and offered a toast. "To good friends reunited and to good friends just made."

Track downed half his glass, and felt the pleasant, customary warmth. He also felt Desiree's fingers in the crook of his elbow....

THERE HAD BEEN MORE TALKING, more drinking and finally, after agreeing to lunch the next day, Track and Desiree had said their goodbyes to Breechmore and his wife and started to leave. The prospect of tomorrow's lunch was something

Track anticipated with mixed emotions. As they were leaving, Pris had grabbed his hand and leaned up to him and kissed him hard on the mouth. Track had kissed her back.

With Desiree beside him, he walked in silence down the steps from the massive house that Track could not bring himself to call a home. Desiree held his left arm with both her hands, her shoulders hunched up. She had said nothing about Priscilla.

He had parked the car himself rather than let one of the valets do it, and they made their way toward it now. As the Mercedes came into view, Track began fishing in his pockets for the keys, watching Desiree as he did. In the cold air, she hugged her folded arms against her chest, the white coat that matched her gown drawn tight around her. "I'll have you inside in a minute," Track said.

"Did you love her?" Desiree asked.

"No, but I made love to her. You gathered that."

"I've never been jealous before."

"You don't have any reason to be now."

"Do you love me?"

"Yes."

"What are you planning to do about it?"

"Marry you. Now get into the car."

"All right."

He opened the door for her, and she eased into the seat.

He walked around the front of the car, un-
locked his side and slid behind the wheel. He
stomped the clutch and worked the gas pedal as he
turned the key. As he had walked around the car
he had done a quick check—both threads he had
placed on the joint between the hood and the
fenders were in place where he had left them. It
was no positive insurance against an explosive
device, but there was no positive assurance of
most things in life, he thought.

"Are you just trying to. . ." Desiree began.

"To what?" he asked, looking at her as the
engine roared to life.

"I don't know. I didn't like the feelings I had in
there."

"I didn't like the feelings I had in there,
either."

"Do you really want—"

"To marry you? Yes. Goes to show how crazy I
am, I guess."

"It isn't just that I love you," Desiree said.
"You know that. I'm a sophisticated woman—I
can handle another woman showing attention to
you. But I like you. She tried to get you to take her
to bed, didn't she?"

"Yes."

"Why didn't you?"

"I like you—that kept me from doing it."

Desiree came into his arms, and Track touched
his mouth to hers. It was hard to be objective, but

aside from everything else she kissed better than any other woman, smelled better, tasted better. Everything was better with Desiree. . . .

IT WAS A TWENTY-FIVE-MILE RIDE, and finally there was a stretch of coastal highway that was straight enough for Track to upshift into fifth. Desiree, beside him, her hand on his thigh, asked, "You didn't like Algie much, did you?"

"Not very much at all."

"He's changed in the three years since I saw him last. It's as if there's something weighing on his mind."

"Maybe spending Pris's money is getting him down. She inherited a lot—she used to say she only went to college and majored in math so she could count her money."

Desiree sounded shocked. "She has a degree in mathematics?"

"Three years at Vassar isn't a degree, but she's got a good head on her shoulders. You know what I mean?" Track took his eyes off the road for a moment and looked at her. "Smart—but she never seemed able to figure out what to do with it."

"I won't say a word," Desiree said with a slight laugh.

"I don't think she's very happy—not at all," Track said.

"Generally or with Algie?"

"Both."

"Then why did you accept their invitation for lunch tomorrow?"

"After what Algie was imagining went on out there on the dance floor while the two of you were in the library, I figured I kind of should."

"What did go on out there on the dance floor?"

Track shrugged. "Pris had her hand on my pants and I threatened to take her dress off."

"All right, don't tell me."

Track laughed. "I just did tell you."

"She what?"

Track looked at Desiree again and gave her his best grin. "I must be irresistible—always been a problem for me."

"Shut up."

Track laughed, downshifting into a curve, up-shifting out of it again. "How fast will your little Mercedes go?" Track asked, looking into the rear-view mirror.

"About a hundred twenty-five miles per hour—why?"

"Look behind us."

When you had seen one Trans Am in jet black with its brights on coming up in the rearview at more than a hundred, you'd seen them all, he thought.

5

Dan Track downshifted into third, double clutching as he did, but the engine roared and the tachometer almost redlined, anyway.

"He's gaining on us," Desiree called.

"Wonderful—does Algie like to drive fast?"

"Algie loves fast driving. But he'd never drive an American car—he collects Aston-Martins."

"Pris is richer than I thought. Hang on." Track fought the next curve, double clutching again into third, then double clutching still again as he upshifted into fourth, hammering his foot down on the gas pedal.

"He's still gaining."

Track upshifted into fifth, stomping the gas pedal hard, feeling himself being pressed back into the seat. He heard the glove compartment opening and shot a glance to his right. Desiree had a Walther P-5 in her hands. He looked back to the road. "You own stock in Walther or Interarms or both?"

"I wish I owned stock in either."

If it had been a movie, he told himself, she

would have been jacking back the slide of the 9mm with a dramatic flair. But it wasn't a movie. "Don't start shooting," Track said. "It might just be some crazy who likes to drive fast."

"Do you really believe that?"

"No, but I wish I did," Track told her lamely, downshifting into fourth, then into third, the tach almost redlining again as the rear end of the Mercedes-Benz 190E fishtailed out of the curve. He upshifted into fourth and accelerated hard, straddling the center line of the highway. The driver's compartment was bright as day with the headlights from the Trans Am reflecting in the rearview mirror.

There was a chance to get up into fifth for an instant and he took it, starting into another curve and double clutching to downshift again, through fourth, into third, riding the clutch a little to get the tach reading down before he gave it gas again.

The Trans Am's engine was audible now, ripping and tearing sounds emanating from it or its exhaust system or both.

Track glanced into the side mirror. He could see a window rolling down. "Hit the floor!"

"My dress!"

"Hit the floor!"

"Merde!"

"Likewise!" A tongue of flame exploded from the passenger side of the Trans Am, and the rear window of the Mercedes shattered. "Does that asshole know how expensive the rear window on a Mercedes is?'' Track shouted. Another tongue of flame lit the night, and a chunk in the center of the rear window blew out.

Track upshifted the Mercedes into fourth, his hand snaking up from the stick shift to slip under his coat and grab the butt of the Detonics Pocket 9. Behind him, the Trans Am closed in on the straightaway. Track stuck the Pocket 9 under his right thigh to keep from losing it and upshifted into fifth on the straight. From the sound of the Trans Am, the standard engine had been upgraded. That it could beat out the Mercedes on the damnably endless straightaway they had entered seemed obvious, inevitable.

Track glanced in the side mirror—the Trans Am was coming up fast. They would fire as they passed. ''You stay down,'' he said to Desiree. ''If they get me. push me out the door and keep rolling—''

''I'd never do that!''

''I'll be dead, anyway, kid,'' Track reasoned, watching the Trans Am. He had a plan, but the timing would be critical or they would get him— and at the speed the Mercedes was holding, even a moment's loss of control at the wheel would send it hurtling off the roadway and into the sea, or into the embankment on the opposite side.

Track double clutched and downshifted into fourth, then double clutched again into third, retarding the clutch as the Mercedes started to drag. The Trans Am was beside him instantly. Track looked to his left and saw a face, an anonymous face. And a riot shotgun.

Track stabbed the Pocket 9 through his open window and pumped the trigger, the little stainless Detonics bucking in his right fist over and over. The shotgun discharged, and Track's eyes were blinded in the muzzle-flash for an instant. The Trans Am was swerving.

Track worked the safety and opened his right fist, letting the Pocket 9 fall to the floor of the Mercedes. Upshifting into fourth, he cut the wheel hard left. "Watch out, Desiree!" he yelled. The Mercedes was heavier, but Track's body still shuddered as his left front fender smashed against the right front fender of the Trans Am. The black street machine fishtailed, and Track cut the wheel hard right, then hard left again, into the passenger door of the Trans Am. The gunman's body was already hanging half through the window, and his head was severed with the impact, cracking into the windshield of the Mercedes.

The Trans Am was veering hard left, and Track cut the wheel of the Mercedes still harder. Sparks flew as metal grated against metal. Tires squealed, and Track's knuckles were numb and his fingers cold as he fought the wheel.

A man was now visible behind the wheel of the Trans Am. Track heard the sharp report of a pistol, and the windshield of the Mercedes spider-webbed.

Track picked up the Pocket 9 and worked the trigger until the magazine was empty. In a jerking motion, the Trans Am spun out, heading toward the drop to the sea. A shriek of metal against metal split the air, and taking the Mercedes with it, the guardrail peeled up like the metal band on a sardine can. Both vehicles were locked together like titans in a death grip.

There was no time. Track dropped the Pocket 9 to the floor again and wrenched the wheel hard to the right, dragging the Trans Am away from the guardrail. The left front fender of the Mercedes ripped away beneath the groaning sounds of metal tearing. Track snapped the wheel left, then right, whiplashing the Trans Am. The black car spun dangerously, its rear end rocketing forward. Track could smell burning rubber and see a spray of sparks as the guardrail twisted around the American car.

And then it was gone, plummeting over the edge of the road. A second later, a black-and-orange fireball raced skyward over the edge of the cliff, searing Track's face as he glanced back.

6

Desiree put a fresh magazine into the Pocket 9 for him while they stopped at the side of the road, and then Track drove the battered Mercedes away from the scene as rapidly as possible, to avoid the police who would inevitably be drawn to the explosion of the Trans Am.

Track pulled the Mercedes into the small garage attached to their villa and climbed out, the Pocket 9 out of its shoulder rig and in his right fist. He looked at Desiree as they walked silently up the driveway. In her fist she held the Walther P-5 from the glove compartment.

"There are two M-16s in the bedroom closet hung up under my mink coat," Desiree said.

"I spotted them last week," Track told her absently.

"What were you doing in my closet?"

"Looking for my sweater. You borrowed it when we had that little cold snap, and I haven't seen it since. What else do you have in the house?"

"Not much. A few more P-5s scattered around

and two Walther MPKs, and of course your personal guns and my little revolver.''

"Any of the servants know where you're keeping these things?''

"I think the maid tried on my mink coat. If she did, she knows about the M-16s.''

"Where are the MPKs?'' Track asked, the gravel crunching under his feet as they walked.

"One of them is taped under our bed—I don't think the maid ever cleans that thoroughly under there. The other one is taped under the couch in the library. I know she never cleans there.''

"How about the pistols?''

"One is taped under the flush-tank lid in our bathroom—I meant to tell you about it. It's sealed in plastic. The others are downstairs, one in the library and one in the hallway and one in the kitchen inside a box of breakfast cereal.''

"What kind?''

"A P-5—like the others.''

"I meant the cereal.''

"Life—I thought that was appropriate.''

"Wonderful.'' Track smiled. They were nearly at the front entrance, and the white villa was almost shrieking out of the darkness in the moonlight.

Track stopped.

"What's the matter?''

"Nothing—just giving anybody in the house a last chance to see we're coming.''

"Why?"

"Why not?" Track said with a shrug. He took one of the Cuesta-Rey Six-Ts from his case and guillotined the tip, then lit it in the blue-yellow flame of his Zippo. "Let's go," he whispered.

Inside him, a sick feeling was growing.

With the Detonics Pocket 9 in his right fist, he started up the stairs toward the doorway, Desiree beside him.

Track stopped on the threshold, waiting, listening.

There were no lights visible in the house.

Track kicked the door. It swung open.

"Dan," Desiree cautioned.

"Wait out here."

"No."

"Wait!" Track ordered. He took a few coins from his pocket and tossed them through the open doorway into the darkness.

There was no shuffle of movement, no gunfire, no sound.

Track went through the doorway with the second small handful of change and flattened himself beside the interior doorjamb.

They had spent more than two weeks in the house and he knew it well enough in the dark. Moonlight was shafting through the open doorway behind him, bathing the long hallway in a gray light.

Track called the maid. "Elsa?"

There was no answer.

Track found the light switch, hit it and threw himself to the floor. He felt something sticky, and squinting against the sudden light, he saw that his hand was touching the edge of a trickle of blood. There was no sound in the house. "Stay outside, Desiree," Track said. But he knew she wouldn't.

He followed the little rivulet of blood to the nearest opening on his left and stabbed the Pocket 9 through the doorway. But there was still no gunfire, no shuffle of feet.

He stepped through. "Holy Jesus," Track whispered, turning away, involuntarily feeling the nausea deep in the pit of his stomach. Walking away from the room, he grabbed Desiree, who was by now halfway across the entrance hall, and dragged her outside.

"Dan?"

Track sank to the steps, leaning forward, his stomach heaving, the hand that held his pistol trembled. He felt Desiree's hands on his neck, her fingers gently touching his face.

"Dan—"

"There's nothing in there you want to see. Believe me."

"But I—"

"Forget it, Desiree. You're better off not going inside that house. Just wait here." Track's voice quavered.

He pushed past her and walked through the

doorway, along the hall and to the first door on the left.

He closed his eyes against it, but he could still see it.

Three bodies were spiked by their wrists to the far wall of the room, the bodies stripped naked, the skin on the legs and arms and the breasts of the two women flayed. Beneath the bodies, pools of blood congealed on the carpet.

The butler. The maid, Elsa. The cook. He had known them only two weeks or so—they had come with the house. They were human beings, skinned alive. Not to make them talk, Track knew, but as an example.

An example from the Master of D.E.A.T.H.

Behind him, he heard Desiree Goth scream, "My God!"

7

Sir Abner Chesterton sipped his sherry. It was a special bottle that the chef at the Waldorf coffee shop kept for him. When in New York, as he was quite frequently these days, he would always lunch at the Waldorf, entering from the main entrance of the hotel and walking through the lobby across the grisly patterned yet oddly beautiful carpet, past the row of shops and down the stairs on the far side of the lobby to the coffee-shop level.

One of the staff would see him, smile and usher him toward his favorite table along the interior side of the restaurant. He had the menu memorized, but always looked at it again. Today, he'd had a light lunch, a club sandwich and rich chocolate mousse. He took another sip of his sherry.

It was the spell of the Waldorf that he loved. One left the street and entered a new world, but it was really an old world, and it was this that made him return again and again.

Going back to his work with the Consortium was satisfying in some ways, but horribly boring after the months behind enemy lines in the Soviet Union and the affair in Acapulco.

He glanced casually at his watch. He had lingered too long over lunch and the e were pressing matters at the office. A rash of rather bizarre deaths was occurring. And there was the controversial mission NASA had planned—should it go wrong it would be the greatest insurance loss in history and bankrupt more than seventy-five percent of the Consortium member firms. And the Consortium's role in the NASA mission's security was his responsibility and his alone.

But it had been a working lunch even though he had been alone. He had made his decision to contact Dan Track in Nice and to contact Track's nephew, George, in New Mexico. The job involved nothing dangerous, just something requiring competence and insight. And surely George would crave some activity by now.

But Track would be another matter. Chesterton took a spoonful of the chocolate mousse. Track was enjoying a well-deserved vacation with Desiree Goth, and to pry Track away for a few weeks would be very difficult. And exceedingly expensive for the Consortium. When George had discussed returning to the Consortium, Chesterton had raised George's salary by fifty percent. George had said he would seriously consider it. To raise Track's salary by fifty percent would bring Track's yearly stipend to one hundred eighty thousand dollars.

But Chesterton knew he needed Track, at any cost.

Chesterton downed the last half inch of sherry.

He stood up, leaving the gratuity he always left and weaved his way through the maze of tables.

He had signed a chit for his meal, and as he walked past the jelly-bean container at the front of the coffee shop he snatched a handful, popping one into his mouth as he passed through the door and started up the escalator. He walked past the shops and into the lobby again, quickening his pace as he headed toward the street exit.

Pushing open the door, he was assaulted by the sounds and smells of the street. Dodging several taxicabs, he made his way across the street with a few other daring souls beside him.

As he passed a shop window, he saw a face reflected in the glass.

He turned and stared—it was the sort of face he had seen many times before on commandos, mercenaries and killers. They all had the look.

"Do I know you?" he asked.

The mouth that dominated the face twisted slightly, and the stranger turned away.

Chesterton walked on, but he hunched his shoulders slightly to assure himself of the presence of the stainless PPK/S American in the shoulder holster beneath his jacket. As he shifted his shoulders, a chill ran along his spine.

He had all the necessary permits to carry a pistol

on the streets of New York, but he was reluctant to take it out of the holster in a city where anyone might have a gun.

Chesterton stopped suddenly. The stranger was less than ten yards behind, still staring at him.

Chesterton looked toward the street. A taxi was moving far too slowly along the curb.

Chesterton slipped his right hand under his tweed sport coat, just as the overcoat the stranger was wearing flew open. Chesterton snatched at the butt of his Walther, but a shotgun was swinging out from under the stranger's coat. He threw himself down, screaming to the people on the street around him, "He's got a gun!"

The shotgun roared, and the window beside Chesterton disintegrated. Stabbing his pistol toward the shotgunner, Chesterton jerked the trigger back. The shotgunner's hand moved to his thigh as his leg buckled. But the shotgun was swinging in a tight arc, the muzzle like a massive creature; for an instant, Chesterton saw himself swallowed inside it. He pulled the trigger of the PPK/S again and again. The shotgun discharged, and in that split second Chesterton thought, "God rest my soul." The pavement less than a yard from his face exploded, bits of it tearing into his face. He fired once more, directly at the head of his attacker.

Chesterton's right hand shook with terror, rage and disgust. The bridge of the shotgunner's nose was lost in a wash of dark red blood as the body slammed against a No Parking sign, then rolled into the street.

The slow-moving cab swung wildly into the street, clipping its left front fender against a hot-dog vendor's cart, and roared away.

Chesterton stood. His knees felt weak.

He looked around, already hearing the police sirens. Off to one side, the hot-dog vendor was yelling excitedly in Spanish and trying to right his cart.

There was still one round left in the Walther's chamber; subconsciously, he had counted them.

He approached the shotgunner and stood over him. His voice didn't sound natural at all to him as he whispered to the dead face, "Do I know you?"

He heard the voice behind him. "Drop the gun, fella!"

8

The seven fountains were lit with yellow light, each fountain spaced perhaps ten feet from the next one, the waters electronically controlled for movement in perfect synchronization. The Master of D.E.A.T.H. walked slowly the length of the long, shallow rectangular reflecting pool, paying strict attention to the dancing waters of the fountains on one level of his consciousness, considering the past twenty-four hours' events on another.

Carlo Capezi was dead. The Cosa Nostra would be upset with him, but it was unlikely that Capezi's successor would aid Dan Track again. The girl who had been with George Beegh was critically injured and if she did not die as the result of her wounds, she would be crippled for life, barring miraculous intervention. And the Master of D.E.A.T.H. did not believe in miraculous intervention.

He hoped he had sent a stiff message to Track and the gunrunner Desiree Goth, killing their servants without attempting to harm the couple.

There was no word from Southeast Asia yet as

to the fate of Goth's confidant and bodyguard, Zulu. But the Master entertained great faith in his Communist Vietnamese friends and their ability to dispense unpleasant deaths.

The one true failure was the botched assassination of Chesterton, the Englishman who was so vital to the Consortium's criminal investigation and antiterrorist activities.

He had wanted Chesterton out of the way not only for revenge but also for economic reasons, a stronger motivation.

He stopped at the fountain farthest from the house and turned back along the path he had taken, walking more quickly. Soon word would be coming of the resolution of another matter of economic importance.

The thought of profit spurred him onward.

9

Her hand was shaking, and Dan Track held it tighter. "If you're right, perhaps we're walking into a trap."

Track only nodded.

Desiree's voice held an urgency that he rarely noticed—she was always so in command. Her Marseilles underworld contacts had arrived and taken away the bodies of the dead servants for burial in some remote area, and others had come to clean the blood from the floors, replace the blood-stained carpet and repair the wall. What seemed like an eternity later, Track and Desiree had called the police to indicate their alarm over the mysterious disappearance of the three servants.

The trashed Mercedes had been hauled away and replaced with an exact match that now stood in front of the house.

Then Desiree had wept for hours. They had gone to bed, made love furiously and she had wept again.

Now they were walking toward the château

where they would meet Breechmore and his wife for lunch.

She said it again: "It might be a trap."

As they followed the butler into the sunlight, she held Track's hand more tightly still. He looked at her; her face was lit with a smile that was positively beautiful, but just as unreal. She didn't look as though she had had no sleep—she looked fresh, exquisite in her pale yellow suit with the straight skirt and the short jacket, in her heels, with her black hair twisted up at her nape. The purse that matched her shoes held her little Model 60 Smith & Wesson.

"Desiree—" Algie said.

She let go of Track's hand, and Algie put his arms around her as she pressed her cheek to his. "Algie, one would hardly guess you were probably up all night," she said, laughing.

Track moved his eyes from Desiree to Algie's wife. She planted a light kiss on his lips. "Too much dancing in the sheets last night," she said in a stage whisper.

Track grinned at her. "No, it's this French climate—turned me into an insomniac."

"I know the best cure for that." Pris smiled again, then she took his hand and led him the rest of the way across the veranda toward a large, round, glass-topped table. A white-coated servant saw to her chair, then to Desiree's. Track sat opposite Desiree, with Priscilla to his left and Algie to his right. The view of the formal gardens was magnificent; all that was lacking was hedges sculpted into the shapes of dollar signs. Money seemed to ooze from the cracks between the paving stones of the terrace.

"I trust you're enjoying France, Dan?" Algie began.

"French drivers scare the hell out of me," Track said with a laugh as he lit a cigarette.

"I'll have the boy take your coat. The sun is warm—I can see you're uncomfortable."

"I'll keep my coat, thanks."

Algie shrugged. "I take it you've had a bad experience on the road. Not on the way here, I hope."

Track flicked ashes into the glass ashtray near his plate. Immediately, the white-jacketed servant removed the ashtray and replaced it with a fresh one. "Last night," Track began. "Darndest thing happened. After we left here, we were driving along and this black Trans Am comes up and nearly runs us off the road. Lucky for me Desiree's Mercedes is pretty fast. We outdistanced him but he must have hit somebody or something, because we went for a drive just to settle our nerves and we passed the same stretch of road later—just driving around, you know how that is—"

"Oh, yes," Algie said as he flashed a smile—but his eyes didn't smile at all.

"Anyway," Track went on, trying to hold his ashes as long as he could to save wear and tear on the servant's shoe leather, "there were cops and wreckers' trucks and even a fire truck. Probably some drunk."

"Probably, yes."

"Dan," Priscilla said. "You should be very careful on the roads here at night."

"As long as that's the only place, I suppose it won't be a problem."

"Well," Algie remarked, "I'm sure a man of your background must have quite a few enemies."

Track looked at Algie and smiled. "No, I don't have a single one, usually at least. Because once I identify an enemy, a real enemy who's out for my blood, well, something always seems to happen to him."

"Curious," Algie said, still flashing his toothy grin.

"Indeed," Track agreed. "But it always seems to happen. No matter what somebody tries, I always get to them."

Algie laughed. "You sound a bit cocky, Dan, if you don't mind my—"

"Cocky," Pris interrupted, laughing with a hollow sound. "In more ways than one!"

"I say—" Algie began.

Track cut him off. "No, it's not false pride or anything like that. I decided long ago that I enjoyed living and there are two ways to go about that. Either let people walk all over you and hope they don't decide to put out your lights, or play rougher than they do.''

"Are you carrying a gun, Dan?" Algie said, clearing his throat. "Is that why you didn't wish to remove your coat? If you are, may I see it?"

"Which one?" Track said with a smile. The Master had been responsible for what had happened at the house, the torture deaths of the three servants. But that had been a warning of what was to come and would have been an exercise in futility if the driver of the Trans Am and the gunman with him had killed him and Desiree before they had reached the house. Track had picked Pris's husband as the money behind the car and the attempt on their lives. "I mean, is there any type that's more fascinating than another to you?"

"A small one—an automatic, I think."

Track pushed his chair back from the table, crossed his legs and drew a Pocket 9 from an ankle holster.

"Rather small, isn't it?" Breechmore said.

"It's just a backup gun, but it gets the job done."

"Then you carry more than one," Algie persisted.

Track reached under his sport coat for the Metalife Custom L-Frame. He set the revolver on the table beside the little stainless 9mm.

"I say, what a lovely piece of work. Your name engraved there in the front—in gold?"

Track nodded.

"What caliber is it?"

"A .357 Magnum."

"Rather on the macho side to shoot, isn't it?"

"Not really. If you had someplace with a safe backstop, I could show you." Track grinned—the ball was in Breechmore's court.

"Ahh, but I'm afraid I don't."

Track hadn't shown him the Trapper Scorpion .45 tucked beside his right kidney, and he had no intention of doing so.

"Hey, guys," Priscilla interrupted.

Track looked at her and started to speak, but Desiree got there first. "You know how men are— worse than children the way they like to show off their toys." Track looked at Desiree and smiled and she smiled back. Track shrugged, and Desiree said, "I think what Dan was driving at was that you're both regular residents here, and we were wondering if you might know somebody who owns a black Trans Am. That car came awfully close to running us off the road. A friend of mine checked the police reports, and they found no occupants in the wreckage and as yet they haven't been able to determine whether the car was stolen."

Track looked at Algie, then at Priscilla. Her face was white and her hands were drawn up into trembling fists.

The voice of the butler drew Track's eyes away from her. "Forgive me, monsieur, but there is a policeman outside who has indicated he has an urgent message for Monsieur Track."

Track grabbed the L-Frame and holstered it, stuffing the Pocket 9 into his trouser band.

Algie was answering the butler, "Show the gentleman in, Andrew."

"Very good, monsieur."

Track eased back from the table, and as he did he caught Desiree's eyes. A word from Algie about the guns and there would be some nasty business with the police officer.

The policeman was coming, following the butler in a long-strided gait, his uniform's razor-edged creases and overall neatness in sharp contrast to his gait. Track stood.

The police officer stopped and saluted. *"Bonjour.* I am Sergeant Richard of the Nice police."

Track tried not to smile. "Yes, Sergeant, is there something I can do for you?"

"I have come on an urgent mission, monsieur. You are Monsieur Track?" Track nodded. "I regret to inform you that your house was broken into and there was violence done there."

Track licked his lips.

"Sergeant," Desiree said.

"Oui, madame?"

"When did this take place? We only left our residence here a short while ago."

"No, madame, the home of Monsieur Track in the United States." He took a leather notebook from his tunic pocket and consulted it. "A Monsieur George Beegh was injured, as was a young woman. The message was received from Sir Abner Chesterton of the Consortium. I have the message here in its entirety." Track took the message form as the sergeant offered it. "My condolences, monsieur."

Track read the cable, only half listening as Desiree talked with the policeman in French too rapid for him to understand.

Dan, George contacted my offices, and I was unable to get back to him as rapidly as I would have liked because of difficulties of my own. Your home was broken into by armed men while George's father was away in Washington and George was entertaining a young lady friend. George was wounded but apparently not very seriously. The young woman suffered severe injuries to her back as the result of gunshot wounds. George's father has been notified, but for health reasons his uncle has decided he should best remain with his associates under their care. I am flying out to New Mexico to join George until you arrive. The reason for my delay was a rather awkward situation in New York. I believe the M.D. may be trying to contact you, as well. Watch that you don't get a chill, Dan.

Track closed his eyes, thinking. M.D.—Master of D.E.A.T.H.? George's father's uncle was the Company. As for catching a chill, Track already knew the Master was trying to contact him. He opened his eyes, saying to the policeman, interrupting Desiree's conversation, "Thanks for your trouble. By the way, how did you know I was here?"

The policeman looked at him, and in his accented English said, "We attempted to contact you through the American consulate and discovered your report with the police last evening concerning the whereabouts of your servants."

"From the police report you learned we had been at the party here last night? Why did you come here?"

"The report stated you had returned from a party at this address, and so we checked here just as a matter of routine police procedure, monsieur. Now there is a question you can answer for me. Is there a connection between the disappearance of your servants and the attack on your American home?"

Track lied. "I certainly hope not. As you may know, Mademoiselle Goth is involved in the export business and I have recently worked as an insurance investigator—one makes enemies in any line of work. I'll certainly inform your office if any information comes to light that would prove useful to your investigation.''

The policeman looked at him, not without skepticism, then bowed to Desiree and Priscilla. He saluted Algie and Track in turn, and said, *"Au revoir*, Monsieur Track. I regret your difficulties.''

"Merci," Track said. He realized he had crushed the note in his fist.

As the police officer left, Track turned to Desiree. She was already making their excuses for leaving before lunch. But Track interrupted her, ''Algie, regarding that black Trans Am last night, we still have to talk about that.''

''I say,'' Breechmore began. ''Are you implying—''

''I'm not implying,'' Track told him. He turned to Priscilla and said, ''It's been good seeing you again, kid. You met George once, didn't you?''

''He must be a grown man by now.''

''Yeah, he is.''

''Be careful,'' she said, and as she looked past him, toward her husband, she thought, be very careful.

Track kissed her on the mouth in a way he hadn't kissed her since they had been lovers years ago. ''You know I'm always careful, kid,'' he said, and he turned and started walking away, Desiree beside him. The click of her heels focused his mind. It had started again. If there was no rest for the wicked, there was no rest for those who combated wickedness, either.

Dan Track kept walking, the note still held tightly in his fist.

10

Zulu held his breath. The leaves beside his head shook slightly and he looked behind him. It was Shin bumping the frond with the barrel of his vintage Colt Official Police. The hand that held the revolver was trembling. Zulu shifted the 870 pump from his right hand to his left and clamped the right hand over the younger man's right wrist to still the trembling and the perhaps betraying frond.

He could hear the sounds of the Vietnamese as they moved boldly through the jungle almost as if they did not care about detection.

The jungles of Malaysia, Zulu told himself, were doubtless quite different from the jungles of Africa—but a jungle was a jungle, and the jungle had been his home as a boy and a young man. It was in his blood.

He found himself smiling. The limited knowledge he had of the Malaysian jungles came from reading the writings of the legendary Frank Buck, who had quested for wild game for zoos and circuses throughout Malaysia until the rumblings of

World War II had made his continuing quest impossible. But a jungle was a jungle and these men, though they might be trained guerrillas, were not born to it as was he. Zulu could feel that in their movements.

He would have been several miles farther along, but for Shin. Though only twenty-five, the lanky Chinese was lacking in stamina. There had been rest stops Zulu had not needed, delays in climbing out of gorges and muddy-bottomed riverbeds. But he would not leave Shin, and had instead taken the enforced rests and slowed his pace to avoid outdistancing the younger man.

And now some of the guerrillas who had attacked their elephant caravan in the jungle the previous day were very close, their AKMs carried sloppily, their web gear festooned with a bizarre, almost international collection of grenades and fighting knives and handguns. Even with the young Shin hindering him, Zulu had successfully evaded the bulk of the force Shin had labeled as North Vietnamese. What they were doing here in Malaysia Zulu could not guess. Unless they had been brought in specifically to hunt him down and kill him. Once he had seen Abdul Kefari, some light would be shed on that—one way or the other.

The men that tracked him now had been one of the scouting parties that had broken off from the main force. Zulu smiled—had he been the enemy leader, he would have assumed his prey to make all haste to the rubber plantation of Kefari. But perhaps a trap waited there, too, and there was no need for interception.

The guerrillas would have to be killed, and their bodies scavenged of whatever food they carried.

The shotgun and the pistol he possessed were his only means to destroy these men.

He looked at Shin, raising his right index finger to his lips in a symbol of silence. Shin nodded his head almost too quickly.

Zulu left the man, moving soundlessly through the foliage that paralleled the animal track serving as a trail, hearing the sounds of the North Vietnamese growing in intensity as they moved through the jungle. For once he wished for an auto-loading shotgun, like Dan Track's SPAS-12.

He gripped the 870 a little more tightly. The magazine tube was loaded with seven rounds of double 0 buck, the chamber was loaded and the crossbolt safety was off.

He moved ahead.

He could hear the North Vietnamese commandos laughing about something, but since he did not speak their language he could not share their joke. He kept moving.

He came to a low, dense patch of broadleafed vegetation and he settled in behind it in a crouch, the Browning Hi-Power in his belt, the hammer cocked, the safety locked. The 870 was in both hands now.

He could see there were six men. They moved too carelessly, almost deserving death, certainly inviting it.

Zulu raised himself to his full height. "Gentlemen!"

He fired the 870, tromboning the pump, firing, tromboning, firing. The 870 bucked hard in his hands as he emptied it into the six. One of them was running, another screaming. One man fired a feeble burst from a MAC-10 submachine gun.

But all six men were down. Two writhed in apparent agony, and another was crawling into the bush.

Zulu shifted the 870 to his left hand and brought the Hi-Power into his right fist, the safety downed as he had drawn it from his waistband. To approach them and slit their throats would have been inviting disaster.

The man crawling into the brush received two bullets to the base of the skull. The crawling stopped. The nearest of the two men who still writhed in their death throes took two bullets in the top of his head. The second one died from two bullets in his temple.

Zulu stepped forward and put a bullet in the base of the skull of each of the other three men.

"Shin, you can come and search these men now."

"Yes, Zulu."

Zulu reloaded the magazine tube of the 870,

chambered a round and topped off the magazine tube again.

He placed the 870 on the ground, propping the muzzle out of the dirt against the body of one of the dead men. Their web gear was ratty, and the knives they carried were rusty. Of the six, one had a decent early-production Gerber Mk II fighting knife with the hourglass taper to the blade. The MAC-10, a .45, was in serviceable if not desirable condition, and there were spare magazines for it. The AKMs were in shameful shape, he thought, a sad end for one of the most ruggedly dependable service rifles in the world. But he selected the least-abused three of the six. He gave Shin a Randall bowie that appeared to have been run over repeatedly by a truck and the MAC to bolster his meager armament.

Zulu rearranged the bodies to belie his true direction, he hoped, then purposely set a false trail for a mile into the jungle before breaking off with Shin behind him for the rubber plantation of Abdul Kefari. And at the back of his mind, Zulu harbored a hidden fear. He named the object of his concern as he walked. ''Miss Desiree.''

11

The Trapper Scorpion .45 and the Metalife Custom L-Frame would never catch up to him in time. Waiting for him in the car Desiree had ordered to meet their arriving jet at Los Angeles airport had been a Randall Service Model .45 and a standard Smith Model 681, the fixed-sight four-inch L-Frame. One Bianchi X-15 rig was like another, the quality always consistent, and that too had been waiting for him to carry the L-Frame. For the Randall he had an Alessi inside-the-pants holster and six spare magazines, plus a good supply of Federal 185-grain JHPs and three Safariland speedloaders for the L-Frame and an equal amount of 158-grain semijacketed soft points. Through a friend of a friend of a friend, Desiree's representative on the West Coast of the United States had secured Track a knife. He had promised it would not be something ordinary, and when Track had taken it from the attaché case in the rear seat of the Mercedes, he had been forced to agree. Called a Fazendeiro, which was Brazilian Portuguese for "farmer" or "rancher," it opened easily and with resounding authority. The drop-point blade was at that delicate happy medium between razor and working edge.

For Desiree there had been a Model 60 Chiefs Special and a box of 125-grain Nyclads. Her armament demands were vastly simpler.

The Mercedes had dropped them at the hospital, and the driver had taken their luggage on to their hotel.

As he walked from the curb, Desiree beside him, she whispered, "Don't worry, this is a very good hospital."

"Chesterton said the girl was nearly dead. George is getting hit too hard."

"If he loves her, and we don't know anything about them together, then he'll still love her no matter what happens."

Track looked at her and smiled. "You're a nice person."

"Don't tell anyone—it would ruin my reputation." She stopped walking and kissed him on the cheek. The click of her heels resumed along the cement of the sidewalk, and Track submerged himself in his thoughts.

The Master of D.E.A.T.H. Vengeance. Against them for foiling the Master's plans in Mexico. Who was the Master? What was the organization D.E.A.T.H.?

"Where's Zulu?" Track asked Desiree as they

passed through the doorway and into the hospital.

"Malaysia. Singapore, then up the—"

"Anything unusual about him being there?"

"He was summoned by an old client and—" She stopped walking. "You think . . ."

She let the question hang.

"Can you reach him?"

"No."

"Can he be tracked?"

"Yes."

"Check it out. Zulu may be in danger."

"If they kill Zulu—"

"Yes." Track kissed her forehead, then started guiding her ahead, toward the counter that had a small sign on it reading Information. He needed more than the smiling candy striper behind the desk could provide him. . . .

DESIREE HUGGED her bare arms to her body. The air conditioning in the waiting room outside the intensive-care unit was apparently too much for the sleeveless, round-necked cotton sweater she wore. Track wanted to give her his jacket, but he couldn't because of the guns he wore.

She smiled thinly at him.

George's face was white with shock as they listened to him. "They just gunned her down—"

Chesterton spoke. "The doctors here are the very best, and of course the Consortium will stand behind you and your young lady, George. She'll have only the best.''

"I asked her to marry me," George whispered, his hands trembling as he tried lighting a Winston. Desiree took the cigarette and lighter from him and lit it, exhaling a thin stream of cigarette smoke through her lips as she passed it back to George. "For the first time," George continued, "I really—"

"George, I—" Track started to speak, but he realized there was nothing he could say.

"I'm gonna get whoever did it." George looked up, his dark eyes hard. "If it was this Master of D.E.A.T.H. asshole, I'm gonna kill him."

Desiree put her arms around him and her head against his left shoulder. His left forearm was bandaged and suspended from a sling. "George— we're praying she'll be all right."

Chesterton murmured, "Yes, George, we all are."

Track cleared his throat and stood up. He walked over to the windows and looked down onto the street, feeling Chesterton beside him after a moment. "L.A. cops know what's going on?" Track asked.

"I thought it best not to mention it. I have private security stationed all around the hospital— two of them are even patients. One had himself admitted for removal of a cyst, the other one lied that he had mysterious pains in his foot. If the

Master tries anything here, it should sound like a war.''

"You're sure it was this Master guy?"

"It would have to be, Dan. Friends tell me it isn't the Russians. If it were the neo-Nazis, there would have been no reason to involve Carlo Capezi—and he was murdered yesterday morning. A car bombing outside his Florida residence. His driver was killed, as well."

Track looked at Chesterton. "The don?"

"Yes. I know you liked him."

"He was what he was, but yeah, I liked him. You know what I mean?"

Chesterton only nodded.

"Couldn't be the Malina terrorists." Track was thinking out loud. "They would have gone after my buddy Lew down in Florida, too. And they wouldn't have had it in for Desiree. And the thing in France—I told you."

"The deaths of the servants, yes. It must be this Master fellow. And he couldn't have picked a worse time."

"Why?"

"NASA," Chesterton began, lighting a cigarette from his case, staring out the window toward the purpling sky. Track watched his friend's eyes.

"What about NASA?"

"There's been nothing about it in the press. After all the flak about the secret military satellite one of the shuttles was launching in the early part of the year, this was kept quite secret."

Track found one of his cigars, guillotining the tip as he asked, "What are you talking about?"

As Track lit the cigar with his battered Zippo, Chesterton began again. "The most complicated mission they've tried. Two shuttles will be readied on the launching pad. The first shuttle will place into orbit two communications satellites, then simulate an emergency that would require a second shuttle launch to rescue the occupants of the first. The second shuttle will launch and go into orbit near the first and effect the 'rescue' of the shuttle team and then launch its payload. Then the drill will conclude and the shuttle astronauts from the first vehicle will return to their ship and both vehicles will come down. Each of the satellites, two on each shuttle craft, is valued in the millions of dollars. If something was to go wrong, the loss would cripple the Consortium member companies who pooled to underwrite the satellites—and the loss of the shuttle craft would be staggering, as well."

Track looked away from Chesterton, watching his cigar smoke deflect against the pale glass of the window. There was no building in easy sniping distance and the thickness of the plate glass would have been detrimental to accuracy, so there was no problem standing there, Track thought absently.

Chesterton spoke again. "If the Master is carrying out some revenge scheme against all those responsible for what happened in Mexico, then it seems likely he might choose to pit himself against the Consortium. It would be hard to imagine a more spectacular way of getting even."

"What do you want?" Track asked.

"I was planning on contacting you and George to get you both involved in the security precautions. But now that's all changed. I can't expose either of you—"

"Why not?" Track asked him.

"I don't understand, I'm afraid."

"Nobody knows who the Master of D.E.A.T.H. is—nobody who's still alive or willing to talk. We can't find the Master of D.E.A.T.H., can't shoot our way into his headquarters or his house or his goddamned castle or wherever he is. And we can't sit around waiting for him to take pot-shots at us. He's already killed Capezi, almost got George and killed or crippled this poor girl, Ellen. He murdered the servants at the house I'd rented—and that was a warning of what he'd do to us. He tried having you gunned down in New York City. God knows if he's suckered Zulu into some kind of trap in Malaysia. And maybe he's even tracked down Baslovitch and Tatiana in their new identities. I'm glad they're out of this."

Chesterton shrugged.

"But we can't just sit around and wait for him to come after us again," Track continued.

"I have a very uncomfortable feeling," Chesterton began.

Track looked at Chesterton and smiled. "This shuttle mission—you think he'd go after both shuttles and both crews?"

"My honest opinion?"

"Yes," Track whispered.

"I think he will, but I don't know how or when."

"How tight are you with the press?"

Chesterton's face brightened with curiosity. "What do you intend, Dan?"

"Let's give the Master something he doesn't want—publicity. And let's force him into liquidating me immediately to avoid any more of it. Find a reporter you trust, someone who really knows his stuff, someone with an editor and a publisher with the guts to print a good story. It's got to be a newspaper the Master couldn't possibly miss seeing—one of the big ones. Maybe he doesn't have his own clipping service," Track said, laughing. "Then I sit down with the reporter and give him an interview. Grab us some headlines. Force the Master to come after me in such a big way that he can't possibly miss. And we nail some of his guys and backtrack from there."

Chesterton stubbed out his cigarette in a pedestal ashtray. "It could work. It could also get you killed quite handily. Quite handily indeed.''

Dan Track didn't say anything. If getting himself killed was the only way to get the Master of D.E.A.T.H., then dying it would be.

12

Klaus Gurnheim inhaled the fresh air deeply into his lungs. Somehow it felt better beyond the walls of his prison. He went into the yard every day that weather permitted, but it was not the same.

He looked at the clean-cut, redhaired federal marshal walking on his right. "The air smells very good."

"Yeah," the marshal answered noncommittally.

Gurnheim looked at the other federal marshal, a woman of about twenty-five. Her hair was done in a pageboy and curled inward a little too much at her nape, making the back of her hair look too short. It was very dark in color. "Beautiful today," he said.

She smiled, but said nothing.

Gurnheim looked behind him toward the van in which he had been transported from the very secret, very high-security prison in the farming country of central Illinois to Chicago.

He had expected the Federal Building, but it was not the Federal Building this time. There was a gigantic, rusted metallic statue in the courtyard. The wind chill was making him feel very alive.

"Why do we go to this building?" he asked. "I thought the FBI wanted to speak with me again."

"The Illinois Attorney General's Office, the Chicago Police Intelligence Unit and some others wish to speak with you, as well. I don't know why they picked here, Mr. Gurnheim."

"I should have made Johannes a nice bomb for this building. It would have gone up so beautifully—all this glass, you know, and so high."

He looked at the female marshal and she looked back at him with disgust. He laughed—it was good to laugh again.

As they approached the glass doors, the doors swung open and Gurnheim caught a strange look in the eyes of one of the three business-suited, raincoated men leaving the building. The look was a look he had seen rarely; he had seen it before in the eyes of the neo-Nazi fanatic Johannes Krieger, and the look had frightened him.

The nearest of the three men swung the right side of his raincoat back, and Gurnheim, despite his wrists being shackled to the belly chain about his waist, threw himself down. He heard the woman marshal shouting, "Pat! He's got a—"

There was a blaring sound. Gurnheim looked up as his shoulder hit the concrete, and he rolled. The submachine gun that had appeared from beneath the raincoat was spitting bursts of flame.

Then there was the sound of a heavy-caliber revolver, and he saw that the woman had a revolver in each fist, firing. The other two raincoated men were firing silencer-fitted pistols.

The woman's body flew back as though it were a discarded rag doll, and Gurnheim looked into her eyes as she fell half across him, her blue eyes cold and dead.

"Up, Gurnheim," the man with the submachine gun snarled, hauling Gurnheim to his feet.

The other two men grabbed him, one on each side.

"Wait a minute," Gurnheim protested. "Who are you? From the Movement?"

"Nazis eat shit," the one with the subgun snarled, spraying it now into the crowd gathering from inside the building. Huge shards of glass fell as the submachine-gun burst cut through the massive plate-glass windows.

Gurnheim was running, the two men with the pistols propelling him along the sidewalk. A large American car jumped the curb and raced toward them. Gurnheim looked behind him. The van the marshals had used to transport him to Chicago had jumped the curb and was cutting diagonally across the square toward them.

Gurnheim looked to his right, over his shoulder again. The man with the insanity in his eyes and the submachine gun in his hands was reaching under the raincoat, and his hand emerged with something Gurnheim immediately recognized—a grenade. The man's hand drew back, his arm extended, then knifed forward. Gurnheim's ears rang with the sound as the explosion rose and fell behind him like a wave.

He looked back at the marshals' van—it was burning and there were bodies on the square around it, some of them on fire. The screams of the dying filled the air.

He was shoved into the back seat of the gray car, and one of the two men with pistols climbed across him, holding him down. The second man leaped in and slammed the door.

As the car started to move, the right front door swung open and the man with the crazy eyes half fell inside, snapping, "Hit it, Ed—damn quick."

"Who are you?" Gurnheim shouted over the roar of the engine.

"Stone Hudson, Gurnheim. I'd just as soon rip your fucking head off, but the guy that's paying me wants it otherwise. You're lucky, you got yourself a job. Making things go bang—just like the old days—"

"But who?" Gurnheim asked.

"Shut up, asshole. You don't need teeth to make a bomb," Hudson warned him.

Gurnheim shut up—he was terrified

13

George Beegh stood beside the bed, watching. More tubes than he had the desire to count led from her nose or to her nose, he wasn't sure which, and to her arms and legs. One came from her abdomen.

"Ellen," he whispered.

He had only three minutes with her, and he used them to watch her. Her face was paler than he remembered it ever having looked. He could not see her hair beneath a surgical cap.

Her breathing was barely perceptible under the oxygen tent.

He watched her.

When her surgeon had left the operating room, the man had said, "Is Mr. Beegh here?"

They had done all they could to save her life. If she lived, it was almost a certainty she would never walk again, have no feeling at all below her waist.

He dropped to his knees beside her bed.

He prayed for her life.

He prayed for the strength to share it with her.

He prayed for the strength to find the Master of D.E.A.T.H. and kill him.

His eyes closed and he felt a hand on his shoulder and looked up. "Mr. Beegh, you'll have to go now," a nurse said.

"It hasn't been three minutes."

"It's been longer, Mr. Beegh. I didn't want to come in and disturb you. But you have to go."

"How's she—"

"There hasn't been any change. If there is, I'm sure Dr. Freeman will let you know right away."

"I mean, she's—" George Wilson Beegh didn't know what he meant.

He stood up.

He stared at Ellen's face.

It was unchanged.

The nurse's hand was still on his shoulder and he looked at her. She was an older woman, but she had pretty eyes and they smiled at him through her glasses. "Everyone is doing the best they can, Mr. Beegh. Dr. Freeman's a very good doctor, a very fine man. He really cares for your young lady, for all his patients."

George tried to talk, but settled for nodding his head.

Then he looked at Ellen one more time and stumbled out into the world.

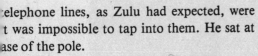

telephone lines, as Zulu had expected, were
t was impossible to tap into them. He sat at
ase of the pole.

'hat will we do, Mr. Zulu?" Shin asked.

'lu looked at Shin. "What would you suggest,
'hin?"

 do not know, sir. It would appear that if we
'deed visit the home of the honorable Abdul
'ri, we may in fact encounter great danger."

'he honorable Abdul Kefari may not then be
 so honorable as we might wish, then,
'?"

'in smiled. "Yes, Mr. Zulu. You are the brave
 I am not."

'hen why did you run to me after the am-
'?"

'ecause perhaps you were hurt, sir."

'nd why did you bring my musette bag and
'hotgun?"

'ecause if you were not hurt, sir, then they
'd be necessary to your continued survival."

'nly a brave man would do such a thing. You

"What are you going to do about this?"

Dan Track looked at Desiree Goth. His arm was around her as they stood by the window. Darkness had pushed away the memory of the sunset, and a yellow streetlight illuminated the street below them. "I'm going to force this Master son of a bitch to come after me."

"Then we backtrack and kill him?" Desiree asked.

"It wouldn't be 'we' if I had a safe place to send you. Where's Zulu when you really need him," Track said with a laugh. And then he said abruptly, "When's your guy in Singapore supposed to get back to you?"

"Not until he knows something. He has the number here at the hospital, the number on the pay phone, the number at our hotel—if we ever get there—and the number of my associate in Los Angeles. When there's word, we'll have it."

"I'm sorry I got you into all this—I mean all of it," Track told her.

"That's what you get for once trying to arrest me and then saving my life."

Track felt himself smile as he looked at her. "Well, I couldn't let a classy dame like you wind up in some terrorist's tent now, could I?"

"You liked me even then, didn't you?"

Track watched her eyes. "No doubt. And you liked me—that's why you didn't let Zulu kill me."

"But I would have, maybe." She leaned her head against his shoulder. "What can we do for George?"

"Nothing but what we're doing now—keep him company until he knows whether Ellen's going to make it. Then we let George help us. He'll want to, very badly."

"Too badly, perhaps," Desiree said.

"For all of it, he couldn't want the Master any worse than I do."

"What would you do if you lost me?"

"I wouldn't care anymore," Track told her quickly. "So don't die—ever."

"Someday I will—someday you will."

Track shook his head. "We're immortal. That old sergeant I had—the one who straightened me out in Germany when I first got into the Army— he'd lost his wife years before. But he told me, 'Track, once you got something like we had, you never die. She's waiting for me. It's just a forced separation. Someday, maybe if you stop this crazy-assed troublemaking, you'll find yourself

the same thing. If you're
looked into Desiree's eyes.
geant Hacker was right, alw
thing. And he was especi
because I found you." He
cheek as he looked back in
feel what was out there—l
him. It always did.

The
cut.
the
"
Z
Mr.
"
do
Kef
"
qui
hm
S
ma
"
bu:
"
my
wc

underestimate yourself, Shin." Zulu stood up, towering over the younger man.

Zulu shifted the position of the 870 in his right hand, raising the shotgun and laying the barrel top strap of the inverted firearm across his right shoulder. "Comrades in arms, what? Now it's time for us to take the initiative. Besides, if I eat any more fruit, I think I'll choke on it."

"To the house of Abdul Kefari, then?"

"Yes." Zulu began to walk, his gait easy. There was no reason to hurry.

Shin fell in beside him. "You see, the honorable Abdul Kefari," Zulu said to his companion, "is a collector of antique aircraft. Because of his remote location, it is necessary that all the items of his collection be flown in. So all the aircraft were at one time at least sufficiently serviceable that a pilot would risk taking the craft airborne. Mr. Kefari does not himself know how to fly. Unless his dietary habits have changed, he is far too rotund to fit behind the controls of any normal aircraft. It is for that same reason that he does not drive. Should Mr. Kefari be in any way connected with our ambush, then we shall kill him. Should he not, then I would say Abdul Kefari is in great, perhaps mortal, danger. And it would be our duty to extricate him from his vicissitude, would it not?"

"Quite, yes, Mr. Zulu."

"It would follow then, that liberating one of his more serviceable-appearing aircraft for our own use would be the logical means to remove our-selves from the jungle. If indeed Abdul Kefari should accompany us, a large aircraft." Zulu made an expansive gesture with his left hand. "If Mr. Kefari dies, then a smaller craft will do. Though I profess no remarkable flying abilities, I believe I should be able to get us up and down again without mishap."

Zulu kept walking. The jungle overgrowth was becoming sparser as they moved into higher lands, ever nearer the house of Abdul Kefari.

16

The eyes of the one called Stone Hudson terrified him. But now Klaus Gurnheim was staring into eyes that were beyond description.

He had looked upon the face of evil many times, but this face—handsome, smiling—this face was beyond all the evil he had known. The eyes were like those of a dead man who had come alive.

"Herr Gurnheim, what a thrill to meet such a person of consummate skill," the owner of the eyes said.

The man extended his hand, and the grip Gurnheim felt was firm, but cold.

"And you are?" Gurnheim said.

"My name does not concern you, Herr Gurnheim. I hope that you are well after your ordeal." And the man curled his arm around Gurnheim's shoulders and propelled him forward along the corridor. There were windows forming the east wall, and he imagined that a few hours ago at sunrise the hallway was full of warmth and light. But now it was lit only by small lamps placed on small tables, and heavy curtains had been drawn across the windows.

"Why did you have me—" Gurnheim began.

"Rescued? I would like to say," the man said as he smiled, "that I was simply doing you a service. But alas, I have an ulterior motive. I required the best man in the world with explosives. You see, my own expert unfortunately died. Now you will assist me."

"To do what, may I ask?" The compliment had made Gurnheim a little bolder.

"To stage the most important explosion ever to occur, in a place where explosions mean life and death. Tell me," the man said as he stopped, "your theories concerning the origin of the universe."

"What?" Gurnheim replied, staring into his host's eyes.

"Surely you are familiar with the Big Bang?"

"The Big Bang?"

"Yes, what began it all. I am not so inflated with self-importance to equate my plan with the origin of the universe, yet there is a marked similarity, as you will see."

"Who are you?" Klaus Gurnheim asked, frightened.

"I am the Master of D.E.A.T.H., my dear Gurnheim, the Master of D.E.A.T.H." And the man laughed.

17

They were staying with George in shifts, which had meant that Dan Track and Desiree had not spent the night together. When he had awakened in the morning after a sleep that classically suited the term fitful, Track missed her warmth. But he had needed to be fresh more than Desiree, and so he had gotten the more enviable of the six hours left of night. He had shaved, showered, washed down a multivitamin with orange juice and chased that with several cups of coffee. The one thing he still missed after years of being away from cigarettes on anything more than an intermittent basis was smoking in the mornings. He could not face a cigar that early in the day.

Track stood in their hotel room looking at himself in the full-length mirror. With the dark blue, vested suit, neither the L-Frame nor the Randall .45 showed. The Fazendeiro hung a little heavily in his suit jacket pocket, but it was all right. He straightened his blue Italian silk tie and was ready.

Track left the room, walked to the elevator and pressed the Down button.

He was pushing forty, but not terribly hard. There was some gray in his hair, considerable gray in the hair on his chest, no gray at all in his mustache. In Russia he had grown his beard out to partially disguise his appearance, and the beard had been nearly white in large patches on his chin.

He thought of this as he entered the elevator, and tried to convince himself that he wasn't getting too old for this sort of life—not yet. But he realized that even if he had to think about it, then he was getting close to the time to quit. He pushed the lobby button and stepped back from the doors. He was vulnerable to attack here in the hotel, with strangers filtering in and out at almost every moment. Chesterton had taken the precaution of posting some private security personnel, trained security specialists.

Track considered that. After this business with the Master of D.E.A.T.H. was concluded, if there was an afterward, the idea of a private security firm—VIP protection and the like—sounded more and more appealing. He was receiving a flat fee of a quarter million dollars to aid in the Consortium's efforts concerning security for the twin-shuttle mission.

It would be enough money to put him over the hump. And then he could settle his life with Desiree. He wanted her out of the smuggling racket.

Track stepped from the elevator and crossed the lobby. Desiree's Los Angeles contact was waiting for him in one of the small seating areas off the lobby, and Track walked toward the man. Short, a bit on the plump side and with thinning hair and wire-rimmed glasses, Wilton Collins looked very little like the agent of the world's most notorious international arms dealer. Track mentally shrugged and thought that it was probably better that way.

Track extended his hand and said, "Mr. Collins."

"Major Track—right on time," Collins replied as he stood up.

"Let's walk," Track told him, and they started across the lobby. "You talk with Zulu much?"

"Oh, quite frequently, sir."

"Good—he told you I was a major?"

"Yes, sir. He had contacted me about you while all of you were in Mexico recently."

"Forget the major part—Dan does real nice. What do they call you?"

"Wilt—sometimes."

"The Stilt?"

Collins laughed. "Hardly."

Track clapped Collins on the shoulder as they passed through the lobby doors and onto the street. "We'll get along just fine." The signal-red Mercedes-Benz 500 SEC coupe was illegally parked, but if Collins didn't mind, Track didn't, either. He climbed in the passenger seat and waited for Collins to get a sufficient break in the morning traffic to get the driver's side door open. The break came, and Collins slid behind the wheel. "Take me for a ride, Wilt," Track told him. . . .

THE CONSORTIUM'S West Coast headquarters occupied the upper floor of one of Los Angeles' myriad bank buildings. Track looked between the slats of a venetian blinds at the smog. It was far too early in the day for air to look that bad.

"Dan?"

Track turned away from the windows. Sir Abner Chesterton, looking very wide awake and dressed in a dark gray vested suit and school tie stood in the doorway of the office. Beside him stood a tall, willowy girl with short curly blond hair and round-rimmed glasses doing a poor job of masking very large, very pretty green eyes. She smiled.

"Dan," Chesterton began again. "This is Holly Morse, the reporter I told you about."

A man wearing faded Levi's and a knit shirt, his body festooned with camera gear, slipped through the door behind Chesterton. "Oh, yes, and this is Miss Morse's photographer, Mr. . . . ."

"Jones. Simple name, but everybody forgets. Call me Harry."

Track crossed the room, skirting the desk and took Holly Morse's offered right hand. "Pleasure to meet you, Miss Morse."

"And you, Major Track."

"Mr. Jones—Harry," Track said as he shook hands with the photographer.

"I understand through my editor that you have a big story for me," Holly Morse began.

"A hard-to-believe story," Track said, looking at her eyes.

"Let me be the judge of that," she answered. "So why don't we get started?"

Track pulled out a chair for her and she moved toward it, sweeping the full skirt of her black dress under her as she sat, crossing her legs, taking out a notebook from her large purse. She set a small tape recorder on the desk beside her, checking the tape as her photographer started laying out his camera gear on the couch at the far end of the room. Chesterton perched on the edge of the desk farthest from Holly Morse, and Track took the desk chair.

"It's Major Track, right?" Holly Morse smiled.

"It was," Track told her, taking one of his cigars from his case and guillotining the tip. "You mind?"

"Not at all—and if I do, I'll tell you about it. Tell me that I have your permission to record this conversation, Major Track," she said as she switched on her machine.

"You have my permission to record this conversation. But if I specify something is off the record, then you must shut off the recorder—agreed?"

She nodded, but didn't smile.

"All right, now you say that on the tape, okay?" Track said to her, lighting the cigar in the blue-yellow flame of his battered Zippo.

"If you say something off the record and request that I shut off the tape machine, I'll do so," she answered.

"Ask away, then," Track told her, exhaling a stream of cigar smoke through his nostrils.

"Give me a little of your background, Major."

SHE WAS ON THE SECOND SIDE of the tape before she stopped asking background questions concerning his military career and his activities since then. He had made her turn off the tape once when she had asked about the rumors that he and Chesterton were part of the team that had infiltrated Russia and become known in the press as the Vindicators. She had agreed that the story, as much as Chesterton and Track had allowed her to know, would not leave the room. So had Harry. But she told Track she was kissing off a Pulitzer. Track had answered, "Maybe this'll get you one instead."

"So tell me about this secret organization you people are fighting," Holly Morse continued.

Chesterton looked at Track and Track nodded

toward him. Chesterton began to answer, "We know very little direct information about it. The name of the organization is somewhat theatrical sounding—D.E.A.T.H."

"Death?"

"It's an acronym, we think."

"You mean like *radar* or *scuba*?"

"Exactly. D.E.A.T.H. is sometimes referred to as the Directorate. And we also know that some fellow who fancies himself the Master of D.E.A.T.H. is its leader. We assume it's a fellow, of course."

"Chauvinist," Holly Morse said with a laugh.

"Possibly," Chesterton replied. "We know for a fact that D.E.A.T.H. was responsible for the attempted and failed demolition of a highly volatile rocket fuel off the coast of Acapulco."

"Tell me about that," Holly Morse said.

Chesterton nodded toward Track, and Track began recounting the events in Mexico, but only those concerning the attempt by D.E.A.T.H. to destroy the supertanker and its potential repercussions on the Mexican government and Mexican-United States relations. "This Master of D.E.A.T.H. guy is some kind of nut, right?" Holly Morse said when Track concluded.

"Most likely," Track told her.

"And how much would his organization have profited?"

"Millions, or billions perhaps," Chesterton cut in.

"So," Holly said, "we have some supersecret organization that just pops up out of the blue and tries to ruin Mexico and make a big financial killing at the same time. Then they attempt to kill you, Sir Abner, and try to kill this George Beegh—" she looked up from her note pad "—and nearly killed this girl Ellen something."

"I'm sorry, George never told me her last name—or if he did I forgot it," Chesterton apologized.

"Why? I mean, this whole thing sounds like—"

"It's crazy," Track said for her. "And maybe it is. What we're apparently facing is an international criminal conspiracy backed by really big bucks. What their ultimate aim is, I don't know. But one concrete thing we did learn in Mexico is that secrecy is one of the cornerstones of D.E.A.T.H. So if you print this story and we can start driving a wedge into their secrecy, we'll start hurting them."

"Now," she said, Track squinting as a flash went off, "these people tried killing several of you—for revenge or whatever."

"For revenge, most likely," Track agreed. "Turn off your tape recorder." She did.

"Fine, then I print this story and try to ignore the fact that they might try killing me or killing my editor."

"Or blowing up your newspaper," Chesterton added cheerily.

"Thanks, Sir Abner," she said with a grin. "But aside from all that, this Master of D.E.A.T.H. person is going to come after all of you again."

"Me, I hope," Track told her, letting himself smile. "If we do it right, anyway."

"Wait a minute—you want—"

"We're using your article to bait the Master into trying again, and very soon. There are some things I want you to print—as much as your censorship or good taste will allow."

"What?" Holly Morse asked very quietly.

"That this Master of D.E.A.T.H. is the leader of a pack of psychos, and that he's the biggest psycho of all of them. That the people he's sent against us were a bunch of incompetent assholes, and we figure that's the best talent he has available. That I know what his next move is going to be and have already taken steps that will—"

The door opened from the outer office and the pretty young secretary Chesterton had been talking to in the outer office when Track had arrived put her head into the room. "Sir Abner, I'm sorry to interrupt, but there's something you and Major Track should know."

Track looked away from the secretary and at Holly Morse. "Off the record?"

"Off the record—what the hell," she said, laughing.

"Go ahead," Chesterton told the young woman.

"The FBI just contacted all the Consortium regional offices. Three hours ago in Chicago, three heavily armed men used explosives and automatic weapons to help Klaus Gurnheim escape from the custody of federal marshals. There were several people killed, including the two marshals escorting Gurnheim. There's no trace of Klaus Gurnheim."

"Who the hell is Klaus Gurnheim?" Holly Morse asked.

Track leaned back in his chair, closed his eyes and massaged the lids with his fingers.

Holly Morse repeated her question. "Who is Klaus Gurnheim? Wait, he's the Nazi who escaped after his conviction in West Germany, and then he turned up in the United States and was incarcerated here, but nobody ever said why."

"Klaus Gurnheim," Dan Track almost whispered, "is a genius with explosives. Totally insane. Probably one of the most dangerous men alive. He fits very well with what we were talking about. There's not a neo-Nazi organization that could spring him and hide him—not in this country. If some earlier ideas Sir Abner and I discussed are correct, he's an instrument for the Master of D.E.A.T.H."

"Wait a minute. . ." Holly began.

Track looked at her, quietly saying, "He's the

mad bomber, the very thing we needed. The very thing."

"My God," Chesterton murmured.

"My God, indeed," Track reiterated. "My God, indeed."

18

"You see, my dear Gurnheim," the Master said, sipping his coffee, obviously enjoying himself. "We have an enormously important project ahead of us. Nothing so self-destructive as the little tasks you performed for Johannes Krieger—"

"You know about Johannes Krieger?" Gurnheim said, surprised.

The Master laughed. "It is my business to know. Hardly a word is spoken in Washington or any of the world capitals that I am not privy to. No, this is nothing like Krieger and his one hundred thermonuclear warheads. What point in being master of a ball of ashes wandering lifelessly in space? No, I intend to own this planet, not destroy it."

"What are you saying?"

"You are uncomfortable, aren't you, with this entire situation. Suffice it to say that I choose to rule a viable world, not a world of total valuelessness as Johannes Krieger's dreams of Nazi supremacy would have wrought. I have experience with Nazis, and I'm sure you're no exception. This irrational obsession with racial superiority and extermination is pure lunacy.''

''But the Jews, they—''

''The Jews? Really, Herr Gurnheim. Some of the greatest artistic, financial, scientific, medical and philosophical minds in history have been Jewish. I have no desire to obliterate anyone but my enemies. None but those who would block the inevitability of my intentions. Working for me shall be quite a bit different for you. And remember, I really do dislike Nazis, so I'd have no compunction at all regarding your demise. But let's look on the bright side. You can have everything you ever wanted to possess. Be rich. Be powerful, if you enjoy that. Whatever you want.''

''But *mein Herr*, what do—''

''What do I wish?'' the Master prompted. ''Very simply put, I need a true genius at blowing things up.''

''But who?''

''The who part of it is totally irrelevant. It is the what part of it. Very soon, NASA will be sending two of their space shuttles into orbit for a rather complex mission. The first shuttle craft will carry two satellites. Before the satellites are launched into their higher orbits, the crew will simulate an emergency. A second shuttle craft, loaded with two more satellites, will then be launched to simulate the rescue of the first crew. After the first crew is rescued, the first two satellites will be launched from the first shuttle craft's cargo bay by means of the remote mechanical arm on the second shuttle. Thus proving that not only can personnel but hardware as well be rescued from a calamity in space. Most commendable. Were the disaster real, the second set of satellites would be launched and the rescued crew returned home. A later mission would be designed to restore the serviceability of the abandoned shuttle craft and fly it back home for a nice, safe landing. The second shuttle will then launch her two satellites and both will fly home in triumph. What a lovely thought, hmm?''

"What is it that you—"

The Master allowed himself to smile. "One of the satellites aboard the first shuttle craft belongs to a company I control. The satellite will be replaced with another identical one that you will load with explosives in such a manner that it will detonate when it must and cannot, by any means, be neutralized."

"But—"

"I understand, Herr Gurnheim, that once the President of the United States held a small pistol to your head."

"Yes." Gurnheim nodded vigorously.

The Master of D.E.A.T.H. allowed himself another smile. "Well then, my dear fellow, look at it this way. If you do not cooperate with me to the very fullest of your abilities, you'll devoutly wish the President had spared you my wrath and pulled the trigger." He reached across the small table to the silver coffeepot on the silver tray. He looked into Gurnheim's eyes. "More coffee?"

19

Zulu ran, his body low, the riot shotgun in both hands. Then he threw himself down and rolled onto his back.

The sun was high and bright.

He rolled onto his side, glancing to check on Shin's progress across the open field.

Zulu looked ahead through the break in the foliage. He could only see part of the house of Abdul Kefari. Zulu pushed his hat back from his forehead, staring, looking for something that would give him some sign. Was Kefari's home occupied? Or was Kefari a willing Judas goat?

Zulu did not look away when he heard Shin skid into the high grass beside him.

"What do we do now, sir?" Shin said as he dropped breathlessly beside Zulu.

Zulu looked away from the house and at Shin's worried dark eyes. "I've seen no evidence of enemy occupation. Therefore, we must take a direct approach. Would you feel competent to fight your way inside and rescue me were the need to arise?"

"What?"

"I said, would you—"

"But I heard, sir. I would try, with all my heart I would try—"

"I know," Zulu said with a sigh. "But would you feel able to succeed?"

"I don't know. I—"

"Then you have just volunteered to present yourself to the honorable Abdul Kefari and tell a tale of exceeding woe regarding my fate. If after a time all seems well, I will make my presence known. If there is trouble, I will get you out. Do you agree? It is your life we risk."

"Is this necessary, Zulu?"

"Yes, I'm afraid it is."

Shin's eyes flickered up and down, then from side to side. Perspiration beaded on the young Chinese's forehead. He unslung the MAC-10 from his body and handed it to Zulu, along with the four spare magazines he had. "I shall keep my revolver," Shin said.

Zulu nodded. "And don't be more heroic than is prudent, Shin."

"Yes, sir." Shin stood.

As Zulu watched, the young Chinese started ahead. If Shin died, Zulu vowed to strangle the life from Abdul Kefari with his bare hands.

20

Shin walked ahead into uncertainty. His mother had warned him that to go to work in the arms business was potentially suicidal. But he had taken the job, anyway. Aside from being rained on, once having three toes broken when an elephant stood on his foot and having to fire his revolver once into the air to disperse a throng of teenage urchins, he had come to no harm. He had been very fortunate.

He kept walking, trying to focus his attention away from his fear, to focus rather on the imposing edifice that was the home of Abdul Kefari. He had seen pictures of such houses. And he knew the story of this house. An American from Georgia whose father had lost his money in the American Civil War had come here in the 1890s, and when he had made his fortune again, some said in opium, he had built this house. It was in the steamboat-gothic style, with gingerbread woodwork, a high second floor and lots of gleaming white paint.

Kefari had bought the home from the half-Chinese daughter of the wealthy Southerner. He'd also bought the daughter's very successful arms trade.

Kefari had expanded the business, and he now smuggled arms, medical supplies, television sets, videocassette recorders and tapes of pornographic movies that were copied in Hong Kong.

But he was said to be a nice man.

Desiree Goth had done business with Abdul Kefari for many years, Shin had been told once.

As he walked, he noticed a series of markers, but there was no fence and no sign of any security people. He imagined that Kefari had some arrangement with the local lawless population that he would supply their needs for various items if they would let him live in safety.

As Shin saw the house in greater detail now, he saw that it was truly beautiful. Stained-glass windows were numerous on both the first and second floors, and a veranda appeared to sweep entirely around the house. Behind the house stood a massive structure of white painted wood that seemed like a long, low barn. A hangar perhaps.

He almost didn't notice the man with the M-16 assault rifle standing on the front porch. "What do you want here?" the man asked in English.

Shin stopped walking and smiled. "I wish to meet with the honorable Abdul Kefari. He was expecting me some few days ago with goods for his much-respected business ventures. I am Shin, the representative of Desiree Goth."

"Wait," the man snapped, then he disappeared through the front doorway. Shin shrugged and waited. It seemed like a long time to stand there in the sun, and he was half tempted to mount the porch and insinuate himself into the shade there. But he did not. After a long time, the man appeared in the doorway followed by an older man wearing a white suit and a fez.

"Hello," Shin said with a smile. "I came to see Mr. Kefari, the honorable Mr. Kefari."

"I am Kefari," the man in the white linen suit announced.

And Shin felt very afraid, because although this man who wore the fez was certainly not slender, he was not grossly fat, either. "It is a pleasure to meet you, sir," Shin forced his voice to say.

"I had expected the great Zulu to be with you."

"Ahh, there was some misfortune, sir."

"Come into my house and have tea or spirits, then we shall discuss misfortune and many things."

Shin's legs were trembling as he started up the steps, and he felt a chill as he entered the shade of the porch. The guard fell back, and Shin followed the man who called himself Abdul Kefari through the doorway. Shin looked back once—the man with the M-16 was right behind him.

The entry-hall door reached some thirty feet up and was crowned with a dark brown wooden dome, the wood gleaming with polish.

Kefari's heels slapped against the polished, mirror-smooth wooden floor.

Shin wanted to run back out the door. Instead, he said, "Your home seems very beautiful, Mr. Kefari."

"Yes, it is beautiful," the man replied.

Shin felt butterflies going crazy in his stomach. "It is a rare pleasure to meet you, sir. I have heard much of your business acumen, and of course I have transshipped much to you over the years."

"And well done, certainly. Where is the black man, Zulu?"

Kefari stopped in front of double sliding doors, waiting for a reply.

"He was killed; I will explain it. And unfortunately your shipment was waylaid, as well. Bandits. Assassins, if you will, sir."

"Ahh, and what has become of the poor fellow's body?"

"Buried, sir—most tragic."

"Yes, come in." Shin watched as his host slid apart the doors and passed through. Shin looked back; the guard with the assault rifle hovered at the end of the hallway by the door.

Shin walked between the half-opened doors.

There was a blur of movement, and something hit him hard behind his knees. He screamed with pain as he started to fall forward, and fists hammered at him. His revolver was wrenched from his hand—he hadn't even realized he was drawing it.

He was unceremoniously flipped onto his back, like a dying fish thrown on a deck.

A jaundiced face leered over him. "You will tell us what happened to Zulu. Your reward will be a quiet painless death. If you lie, I will know and I will punish you."

"Kefari—what happened to him?" Shin asked, his voice rigid with fear.

"Kefari is dead. Where is Zulu?"

21

George Beegh sat down as Dr. Freeman had asked him to do.

"Mr. Beegh, I wanted to talk with you about Ellen Mansfield."

"How is she?"

"Well, her vital signs are strengthening. But there's the other thing. Now, no doctor can see into the future, you know. We don't have crystal balls or anything like that."

"What are you trying to tell me?"

"You can never be certain these days—we're always learning more. Do you know much about anatomy?"

George felt suddenly angry. "I can find my ass from a hole in the ground—sorry, I—what's wrong with her?"

"In layman's terms, she's paralyzed from the waist down. And unless there's some new surgical procedure developed Ellen will never have any feeling below her waist—*any* feeling."

George wanted to punch somebody in the face, hard.

The doctor was still talking.

"She'll never walk again, at least that's my prognosis. Now you can take her elsewhere, call in other doctors—whatever you like, really—and I'd be just as happy as you are if there's some possibility I overlooked."

"Jesus," George whispered.

"She's a very young woman. And you're a very young man—you both have difficult decisions ahead of you. I mean, well, the lower part of her body is still alive, but it's useless to her." The doctor stood up, looking uncomfortable.

"You're saying I could never make love to her," George supplied.

"Well, I'm not saying that, but it would be rather one-sided, if you get my meaning, Mr. Beegh. I gathered you two were very close."

"So I should just hang around until she's out of any danger and then just run away—"

"I can't say that, but it might be best."

George reached under his blue denim jacket and drew the Smith & Wesson 469 Mini-Gun from his shoulder holster. He pointed it at the doctor's heart. "This thing is aimed at something that's just like Ellen's lower body—no feeling."

George put the gun away, then turned and walked down the corridor.

He wasn't going to let the man see him cry.

22

"Resting, is he?"

"Yes, sir," Stone Hudson responded, walking beside the Master of D.E.A.T.H. down the length of the reflecting pool.

"Gurnheim should be watched very carefully. He's quite insane."

"Yes, sir." Hudson nodded, but he thought it was the pot calling the kettle black.

"You have a flair for bloodletting, Colonel Hudson."

"You want to make an omelette you got to break a few eggs, sir," Hudson responded, lighting a cigar.

"Yes, I suppose you must. Let's discuss this man Track, shall we?"

"Yes, sir. You give the word and he's dead meat."

"How reassuring you sound. I recall our late mutual acquaintance Mr. Beal sounding similarly confident."

"Beal was a wimp, sir, worried about his family, shit like that. He wasn't into this because he wanted to be."

"And why are you into it, then?" the Master asked. The Master appeared to be studying the sunset. It was lovely, Hudson thought.

"I figure you just might pull this off, and if you do, you'll be the first person since Augustus Caesar to rule a civilized world worth ruling. But it isn't easy to keep power. You'll need somebody just as—" Hudson stopped, trying to think of a word that wouldn't offend.

"Ruthless?"

He looked at the Master. "Yes, sir, if you like."

"Let me say, Colonel Hudson, that if you are as successful in all your missions on my behalf as in the rescue of Klaus Gurnheim, you'll be justly rewarded. And of course you'll also be very dangerous to me."

"How is that, sir?" Hudson asked.

"You'll possess enough information to damn me, won't you?"

"To damn us both, sir."

"Yes, quite. It has come to my attention that Track has given a story to one of the more prominent West Coast newspapers. I want the printing plant destroyed—as a warning. And I want Major Track eliminated permanently. I was playing with him when I had your men leave that little warning in France. But he's ceased being anything more than a nuisance."

"I met Dan Track once a couple of years ago," Hudson said. "He didn't seem so tough. He's a good man with a gun and with his hands, but he doesn't have the heart of a killer.''

"Heavens—you mean we're up against a truly good man?''

Hudson laughed. "If you want to call him that, I suppose so. He used to support his nephew and his sister. Never been married, and since he started running around with that bitch Desiree Goth I hear he's even stopped chasing.''

"You seem to know a great deal about Track, having met him only once.''

"When I met Track he was teaching officer-survival skills to a police department in Africa. The people I was working with were out to kill the police. Different sides of the same coin. I pegged this Track guy right away, checked out his service record, kept tabs on his activities. My guess is he was one of the Vindicators, those guys who were giving hell to the Commies a while back.''

"He was,'' the Master said, stopping his walk, turning and starting back along the reflecting pool the way he had come.

"He's got guts, I'll say that. But he plays out of his league. You can't do what he does and be so fucking goodie-goodie. I mean, hell, if I'd been playing war inside Russia I would've—''

"I'm sure you would have,'' the Master said sharply, cutting him off. "Tell me more about Track—not his exploits, but his character.''

"I did my homework after you sent us out to do

that number on the servants at the house Track
and the Goth woman were sharing. He's a funny
guy—goes out of his way not to kill, but he's done
his share. Patriotic like you wouldn't believe. Real
attached to Desiree Goth, to that nigger who's her
bodyguard, to that Brit Chesterton and to that
nephew of his. Even got tight with that former
KGB agent named Baslovitch.''

"Yes. No luck finding Baslovitch and the
woman yet?"

"None, sir," Hudson admitted. "But I've got
men working on it."

"Tell me more. How is he most vulnerable?"

"Hell, we could put the bag on his nephew or on
Desiree Goth—that's a good bet. Zulu should
be dead by now. The ambush went okay, but Zulu
and some other guy got away. The people I hired are
tracking them through the jungle. We should get
that nigger anytime now."

"Splendid. You mean kidnap this nephew or
the woman and force Track into our hands?"

"We could, sir, but it would be better just to
gun him down and be done with it."

"The direct approach." The Master nodded.
"All right, do that, after destroying that printing
plant."

"I'll take care of it personally, sir," Hudson
said. He chewed down hard on his cigar.

"No, no, you won't. Have it done by your best
people. I need you here. Nothing can go wrong

with this operation against NASA. Crushing the Consortium should be quite useful to me, financially as well as spiritually."

"I can do it and be back, sir—"

"No. That's my final word on it. Order it done, and right away."

The Master walked off and Hudson stood looking after him. Beal had been weak, but Beal had also been right. The Master was scary, crazy.

He started to walk toward his own office at the far end of the estate's main house. There was much to do.

He had some people in mind who could take care of the printing plant, and he had some likely candidates to take care of Track.

He had to get Track alone, he thought, or with the Goth woman. Maybe six men, with automatic weapons.

And Dan Track would be one do-gooder who had done his last. Hudson lit a fresh cigar for that one.

23

He had experienced pain before, Shin told himself. And they were just hitting him, after all. The worst was yet to come.

It would have been easier if they had allowed him to double over and absorb the shock as they hammered their fists into his abdomen. But the hands that held his head back would not allow him to double over.

In front of him, when he kept his eyes open, he could see the partially burned body of Abdul Kefari. Kefari had apparently been a brave man.

Either that or his tormenters had merely delighted in his pain.

It was a sobering thought. Would they merely kill him or would they burn him?

He tried not to consider the latter.

His face was slapped and he heard his host ask again, "Where is Zulu?"

Shin gave the same answer. "He is dead, as I have told you. No amount of beating will bring him back to life." He had told them that Zulu had been mauled by a tiger. He had forced himself to visualize the tiger and Zulu locked in deadly combat, the location of the tiger's wounds.

"He is not dead—he would not die so easily."

"He is dead, and he did not die easily. He fought bravely but was overcome," Shin contended.

He felt a knee smash into his crotch, and he screamed like a baby and realized that he whimpered.

"Where is Zulu?"

"The tiger killed him! I buried him! I could take you to the very spot where—"

A fist hammered into his mouth and again he could taste his own blood.

"Where is Zulu?" his tormenter shouted.

"Here, gentlemen," Shin heard a familiar voice say.

For a moment, everything was quiet. Shin looked up. In the window, at the far side of the dining room that had been converted into a torture chamber, riot shotgun in his right hand, stood the mountainous form of Zulu. "Would any or all of you care to try hurting me?"

Shin wanted to laugh with joy.

The man with the jaundiced face turned to face Zulu, and the white-suited man with the fez drew a pistol. But the imposter made no move to fire. Shin turned his face toward the guard with the assault rifle. He wanted to do something, but he was beginning to drown in a sea of pain.

The jaundiced man was talking, and Shin cleared his head and listened. "I have more than a dozen men. You cannot escape."

"I have no intention of escaping," Zulu replied evenly. "By the time I leave here, there will be no one alive to escape from."

"You're a dead man!" the man in the fez screamed.

Zulu's voice rang from the window with low, growling laughter. "Then tell me, since dead men tell no tales, who ordered this?"

The jaundiced-faced man sneered, laughing suddenly. "Colonel Stone Hudson."

"The mercenary assassin. And who is paying the bill?"

"Hudson said it was the Master of D.E.A.T.H. Do you know him?"

Zulu's low, roaring laughter came again. "Not presently, but I will correct that social oversight. But first—" The riot shotgun swung upward and Zulu leaped down from the high window. The P-38 in the hands of the counterfeit Kefari fired twice. The riot shotgun roared once. Zulu rolled across the floor, the riot shotgun firing again and again, the body of the jaundiced-faced man rocking once, rolling back, skidding across the floor.

The guard was firing his assault rifle. Zulu's riot shotgun fired, and Shin's ears rang with the stereophonic cacophony. The riot shotgun bellowed again. Shin screamed against the din of gunfire.

The guard was down on his knees, his assault rifle gone, both hands pressed against his abdomen, blood oozing between his fingers.

Shin looked up. Zulu, the riot shotgun shifted to his left hand, the Hi-Power in his right, was walking toward him, and Shin sagged against the ropes that bound him. Zulu said, "My regrets, Shin, at not arriving sooner. But I was detained silencing the rest of the men outside. Only these two—" Zulu gestured toward the jaundiced-faced man and the guard who held his intestines in "—remain alive, and I guess it's time to correct that last little detail." Zulu raised the pistol and fired one-handed like a turn-of-the-century marksman. A bullet hit between the eyes of the guard, and the body flopped back. Another found a home in the side of the head of the jaundiced-faced man, and the left temple blossomed with blood.

Shin felt his body held tight against Zulu's chest. Looking up, he saw a knife blade slashing through the ropes that bound his wrists above his head. Then the awful pain in his shoulders and arms took on new meaning. He felt himself being lowered to the floor. "One thing, Shin," Zulu was saying, his voice low. "Never fault your bravery ever again. It would be a hideous lie."

Shin tried to speak, but couldn't. He felt it was safe now, and he closed his eyes.

24

Melchior Brown huddled in the corner away from the light that illuminated the loading-dock area. He thought about Hudson. Hudson disliked blacks intensely, yet he hired blacks to do his dirty work.

Brown looked beside him and saw Teasdale, Hollings and Boles, their faces sweating despite the fact it was not a warm night. Teasdale rasped under his breath, "Shit, what the hell we waiting here for?"

"For the security guard, asshole," Brown muttered.

Brown closed the fingers of his large black hand on the pistol grip of the Barnett Trident crossbow. He could hear the click of the guard's heels on the pavement, smell the tobacco of the man's pipe. Brown tucked back deeper into the shadows, waiting.

"Do it, man," Teasdale rasped.

Brown didn't answer, closing his fist tighter still on the crossbow pistol.

The security guard's pipe tobacco was stronger smelling now. The click of heels stopped.

Brown stood up. He called out, "Hey—old man!"

The security guard turned around, and Brown extended the crossbow pistol at arm's length and pulled the trigger, feeling the slight drawing-forward motion as the bolt launched. The guard's hands went to his neck, and his body twisted in the alley light as it fell. Then the old white man was lost in the shadow.

Brown was running, circling the cone of yellow light, staying in the shadow, a revolver in his hand. He skidded to his knees beside the guard. The man was still alive. A few twists of the bolt in the neck fixed that.

Brown took the guard's pistol. He didn't know anything about guns except how to shoot them at close range; it was all he'd ever needed to know.

He heard the scuffing sounds of tennis shoes on pavement, and looked up to see Teasdale, Hollings and Boles, laden with their sacks of cotton batting and cannisters of gasoline.

Brown searched the dead guard's body and found his keys. "Let's go," Brown announced, up from his crouch, running toward the loading dock.

"YOU SURE YOU'RE UP TO THIS?"

"Yeah, I'm up to this."

"Okay," Track said. Chesterton stopped the Mercedes and cut the engine. They had driven the last half block without lights.

Track got out on the opposite side, the SPAS-12 slung under his raincoat. His guns had arrived an hour ago, and the Trapper Scorpion rested beside his right kidney, the Metalife Custom L-Frame snug under his left shoulder. The Randall .45 was thrust into the waistband of his trousers.

Track crossed around the front of the Mercedes' hood, looking back once as George climbed out. Chesterton carried the attaché case with the Walther MPK subgun and the spare magazines, in addition to a stainless PPK/S American. George, too, carried extra armament, including a military model folding-stock stainless Mini-14, slung under his trench coat.

The printing plant was across the street, lit by yellow industrial lights. A high chain-link fence surrounded it, and there was a guardhouse a hundred yards to Track's right where the main gates were located. "Let's go," Track whispered. Chesterton fell in on his left, George on his right.

"Why the hell didn't we just drive up to the gates?" George said.

"I figured the walk would be good for us," Track responded.

"They may have already entered the printing plant," Chesterton said in a low voice. "I hope we've arrived in time."

Track stopped in front of the gates; they were locked with a padlock and chain. But as he rattled the gates, no one emerged from the guardhouse.

"If there's a guard in there, he's deaf or he's dead. And this padlock's been—" Track shook the chain again and the lock fell to the pavement "—jimmied."

Track uncoiled the chain from around the gates and pushed them open. He glanced behind him, and George brought out the Mini-14 from under his trench coat. "Put her on full-auto, George."

"That's where she's at, Dan."

Chesterton, his pistol in his right fist, rapped the butt against the guardhouse door. "Deaf or dead—yes," Chesterton murmured.

Track turned the knob and pushed the door open. Shoving the SPAS ahead of him, he stepped into the guardhouse. On the floor lay an old man wearing a security guard's uniform, his holster empty, a crossbow bolt protruding from his neck. There was a pool of blood on the floor beside him, and a thin line of blood leading to the door. "We're too late. They're inside."

Track ran from the guardhouse and started across the parking lot toward the two-story building that housed the presses—and the forty-three people who worked the night shift....

BROWN HAD DISCARDED the pistol crossbow and now held one of the four MAC-10s Hudson's buddy in L.A. had provided for the job. Brown had no intention of giving them back. Hudson would threaten, but the MACs would bring maybe two thousand apiece to some people he knew who liked to rob banks. He might even take that up himself.

"All right," he shouted, "keep movin'!" The eighteen employees he and Teasdale had rounded up were scared, and Brown liked that. That more than half of them were black and he was about to kill them didn't concern him to any great degree. Teasdale ran ahead. Hollings and Boles had already herded about two dozen men and women into the chain-link cage at the far end of the second floor. "Keep movin', dammit, or I'll start shootin' you mothers!" The eighteen men and women moved a little faster.

Brown looked upward and saw the skylight. If he shot a few holes into the glass and brought it down, the place would go up quicker because of the updraft. He made a mental note of the idea. "All right, listen up," Brown sang out. "Teasdale, you and Boles start layin' out the stuff. Hurry up and get it. Hollings, you watch the folks. Anybody moves, kill 'em."

Brown turned away and started back across the work floor toward the freight elevator. Everything had already been laid out for the fire on the first floor—the gasoline, the cotton batting, the jellied gasoline they had made up. It would look like a regular arson job, and that was what Hudson had ordered.

He pushed the elevator call button and waited.

He wanted one last look around on the main floor
where the presses themselves were housed. He
would come back up and make sure Teasdale and
Boles had done their work. Then they would set
the candles and run for it. After shooting out part
of the skylight. The updraft was a good thought.

The elevator door opened, and there standing in
front of him was a white man, and the biggest
shotgun Brown had ever seen suspended on a sling
across the man's body and under his right arm.
The man's hands were empty. The white man had
a mustache, and all he said was, "Hi!"

"Who the fuck are you, man?" Brown realized
his hands were shaking a little as he held the
MAC.

"Lay down your weapon and tell your guys to
do the same."

"Fuck off, man! Shit—what are you—some
kinda goddamned comic-book hero? They's four
of us with submachine guns, sucker."

"You count real good," the white man said
evenly. "I got you outnumbered."

"Where? Don't gimme no crap about cops sur-
rounding no building, you jive?"

"No cops. I've got two friends downstairs disarming your little firebomb. I don't need any help
to take care of guys like you."

"Shit, man—"

The smiling white man opened his suit coat
slowly, and Brown could see the butt of some kind

of automatic pistol gleaming dully against the dark blue of the man's vest. "Big deal, honkie! So you've got a shotgun and a lousy handgun."

"Yeah, well, all I'll need is the shotgun, most likely. Now, one last time." The man's hands didn't move. "Put down the squirt gun and tell your little buddies to do the same—okay?"

"You're dead, sucker."

"You're mistaken," the white man replied with a smile. Brown started moving the MAC-10 up on line. The man's right hand was moving—the shotgun was coming up. Brown started to pull the trigger on his submachine gun, but he couldn't hear anything. There was a blinding flash of light, and he felt the way he'd felt the time he'd gotten clipped by a car and been thrown back up onto the curb. Everything went black.

25

Dan Track broke into a dead run from the elevator, past the body of the gun-shot man. One of the men near the chain-link cage was shouting something to the two other men who were well past it now. Track didn't take time to listen—he pulled the trigger on the SPAS once, then once again. He'd loaded the magazine tube with slug loads. The man beside the cage went down, his subgun firing wildly skyward. Track ducked back beside some packing crates as chunks of glass tumbled down, shattering on the concrete floor. "In the cage—look out for the glass!" Track shouted.

When the glass stopped falling, Track started running again, toward the two men at the far side of the building. A burst of submachine gunfire from one of them caused Track to draw back beside another stack of crates. Slivers of wood from the crates blew out into the room. He stabbed the SPAS around the corner of the crates and fired twice.

He tucked back, shouting, "You people in the cage—get down!" He fed more slug loads into the magazine tube, running across the open space between the packing crates and the cage now, flattening himself beside the cage as more of the subgunfire hammered toward him, skipping across the cement floor. "All right, get back!" Track leveled the .72-caliber muzzle of the SPAS at the cage door's lock, firing once. The Federal Super Slug ripped the entire lockplate out of the door and hurled it to the rear of the cage. "Stay inside until I go past you!" Track shouted to the men and women in the cage. "Then run like hell for the back stairs and don't stop till you hit the parking lot!"

Track pushed away from the cage and ran toward the front of the building, toward the two subgunners. He wanted one of them alive if he could swing it—but he wanted them one way or the other....

GEORGE BEEGH WAS TAKING THE STAIRS at the front of the building two at a time, the stainless Mini-14 in his right fist. Chesterton was blocking the back exit with the Walther subgun. George kept moving. He'd heard the reports of his uncle's shotgun, heard the bursts of subgunfire. They had gotten closer to his stairwell each time. Now he could hear running footsteps on the stairs above him.

George stopped moving, waiting, the Mini in both hands at hip level. "Come on," he muttered under his breath. "Please—come on."

He saw a figure hit the landing and turn down the stairwell. George fired the stainless assault rifle, and three 3-round bursts of .223 hammered into the anonymous gunman. The body tumbled back, the subgun in the man's hands firing upward into the stairwell. George fired another 3-round burst, and the chattering subgun fell down the stairs as the body stopped flopping around.

"George!"

"Dan!"

"How many you get?"

"One—nobody got past me."

"There's one on the roof then—I'm taking him," Track called down.

George sagged against the wall. He looked at the gun in his hands and closed his eyes for an instant. . . .

DAN TRACK TOOK THE LADDER upward, toward the open roof hatch. The SPAS was fully loaded and dangling across his back on its sling. The Randall .45 was in his right fist, the hammer at full stand, the safety off.

If the fourth subgunner was smart, he'd stay near the roof hatch and wait. Track hoped the man wasn't smart.

Track kept moving up the ladder.

When he was nearly at the top, he upped the safety on the Randall and reached into his trouser pocket and found a handful of change—it had worked before. He lobbed the change through the roof hatch, then vaulted after it, going into a roll through the hatch opening as subgunfire tore out of the darkness. The Randall .45 was back in his right fist, and Track downed the safety and pumped the trigger, emptying it toward the muzzle-flashes as he crawled behind a heating-vent stack. Track stabbed the emptied Randall into his trouser band, the slide run forward. He grabbed the Trapper .45 and downed the safety, shouting into the darkness, "Hey, fool! You still alive out there?"

"Come and get me, you damn honkie cop!"

"Just throw down your gun and I won't kill you. I want to talk."

"Go to hell, man!"

"You'll beat me to it if you don't throw out your gun, man!"

A frightened-sounding voice came back from the darkness, "Come and get me!"

Track said to himself, "I was afraid you were going to say that." Track edged out from behind the vent, the darkness on the rooftop total except for a gray sheen from the partially shot-out sky-light that dominated the roof's center. He could hear police sirens in the distance.

He threw himself into a dead run for the next vent. Subgunfire rattled from the darkness near the skylight, and Track wingshot three rounds from the Trapper .45 toward the sound as he ran, finally throwing himself down behind the vent.

It was always possible the man would run out of ammo. But the two dead men Track had seen had each carried two spare sticks in his belt. They'd started out with more than ninety rounds apiece. "Hey," Track shouted into the darkness. "Either throw out your gun or I'm coming in to get you—I don't have time for this shit!"

There was a burst of subgunfire and Track was up, the SPAS-12 in his hands. Track fired it into the darkness as he ran near the skylight.

There was a flash of gunfire, and Track could see movement, a human shape, careering out of the darkness and toward the gray of the skylight.

As the body hit the glass—a moment that seemed to appear in freeze frame—Track skidded on his heels, lurching as he changed directions, just stopping himself before hitting the skylight.

He stood there, looking down. It was at least thirty feet to the floor.

The body lay twisted and broken in the shards of glass.

He could see George moving toward it, then bending over the body. George looked up and, without emotion, shouted, "The fall didn't get him—it was the two slug loads in the chest."

"Wonderful," Dan Track said into the darkness.

26

The only one of the aircraft—twenty-eight in all—
that seemed serviceable was, to Zulu's dismay, the
oldest one. "You know, Shin," Zulu remarked,
"if memory serves, and indeed it usually does
quite admirably, this is a World War I vintage aircraft."

He looked back at Shin. The young man sat on
the lid of a wooden tool chest, still holding his abdomen. "I believe it's a DH-4," he said. "When I
was a little boy, I loved airplanes and read all I
could about them. The colors are right for a
DH-4, in any event—they came from the factory
painted khaki and cream color."

Zulu came closer to the biplane, gesturing toward something that looked like a small generator
slightly aft of the midway point between the two
cockpit openings, just forward of the drawing of
the Statue of Liberty. "A generator?"

"The DH-4s were used for artillery support;
that's a wind-driven generator that operated their
radio."

"Ingenious," Zulu said. "I don't suppose your

interest in vintage aircraft extends to flying them?"

"I don't know how to fly, sir."

"Well," said Zulu as he patted the portside fuselage, though not too vigorously for fear of punching a hole in it, "this is the only one whose tires appear not to have dry rot. Now we have to get it going."

If they didn't get airborne soon, they would never get airborne at all. There had been a radio in Kefari's dining room, a radio brought by Kefari's tormenters and murderers. While they were there, a signal had come in from the ambushers. It had been clear signal, obviously from a transmitter that was close by. For once Zulu considered lack of knowledge an asset—had he understood Vietnamese, he might have been too discouraged to try getting airborne at all.

THEY HAD TAPED the crumbling wiring for added insulation. The de Havilland DH-4 with a Liberty engine had been stripped of its original armament, and Zulu had improvised. From Abdul Kefari's collection, he had liberated two German MP-40 submachine guns and a large amount of 9mm parabellum.

Shin sat aft in the gunnery position, Zulu in the cockpit at the controls. Starting the machine had been surprisingly easy. Zulu edged the craft forward through the hangar doors and into the diminishing sunlight. He was almost feeling confident, but as soon as he was clear of the hangar his mind changed.

"Shin!" Zulu shouted over the engine's roar. "Our enemies are upon us!"

About two dozen men were running across the open field from the direction of the jungle.

As assault-rifle fire tore toward the plane, Zulu began playing the flaps to turn the aircraft into the wind. Trouble was, the wind was coming from the direction of the charging force of men. "We must fly toward them in order to take off," Zulu shouted. "Mr. Shin, may your aim be true!"

Zulu started throttling out the biplane, and the slender air frame trembled and groaned.

He could hear the submachine gunfire coming from behind him as Shin returned fire at the Vietnamese. Zulu doubted the effect of the MP-40 and its 9mm solids at such a range, but if it would serve to discourage their attackers even slightly, he had ammunition to burn.

He was closing in on them now, the distance less than a hundred yards.

The MP-40s hummed from behind him. The wind tore at him. After a long burst of subgun fire from Shin, two of the Vietnamese attackers were down.

Zulu concentrated on getting the old plane airborne. The ground speed was increasing, and ahead of the DH-4, a half dozen of the Vietnamese were forming a human blockade, their assault rifles to their shoulders. The MP-40s were out of synch with the prop, and to fire straight ahead would have turned the blades into matchsticks.

He throttled forward all the way. "Here we go!"

Assault-rifle fire pinged off the DH-4's body frame. The aircraft bounced and jolted across the field, the engine screaming. They lifted then fell, then lifted again. They were airborne.

Shin shouted, "We've made it!"

Assault-rifle fire continued from the ground beneath them. Zulu leveled, correcting his altitude, then beginning to climb. "What do you say we strafe them a bit, Shin?"

Shin shouted to him against the slipstream, "I'm with you, sir!"

Zulu took the plane into a steep bank and headed back over the field. He leveled off just out of range of his attackers. Then he brought the biplane's nose down and throttled out, skimming the ground a hundred feet over the terrain. The Vietnamese assassins scattered as subgunfire roared from the aft cockpit. Bodies fell, tumbled and were still. It was a rout, and Zulu screamed at his enemies, "Victory is ours!"

He banked out of the pass and went into a steep climb. Then he throttled back, and the aircraft dropped suddenly as he prepared for another pass at the field.

A half dozen men remained alive.

"Again, Mr. Shin!"

"Again, Mr. Zulu!"

He liked Shin—there was spirit in him, courage. He would have made a good warrior.

Zulu throttled back, leveling off at seventy-five feet. The subguns roared again, and the bodies of their enemies were driven before them as they were struck with death.

When the enemy was vanquished, Zulu began climbing the DH-4 into the low clouds that were orange tinged by the setting sun.

Now there was Stone Hudson.

27

Dan Track was alone. He had virtually forced Desiree Goth into the company of Sir Abner Chesterton and George. It had to be that way. The news of the aborted destruction of the printing plant would have reached the Master of D.E.A.T.H. soon after it happened—Track was convinced of that. And the sheer fact that an operation had been set in motion against the printing plant had convinced Track that an operation had been set in motion against him.

He had lingered longer with the LAPD than any of the others, and he drove the Mercedes now, taking himself up into the residential area near the Hollywood sign. Stars from the entertainment world lived there, their houses nestled amid winding streets. Track turned the Mercedes from one street in to another.

He was being followed, but at a considerable distance. He had detected the same light pattern behind him too often for it to be anything else. But the distance was too great for a conventional tail. Which meant that the Mercedes had been wired. Out of some sense of perversity, he had decided to give his tail a nice complicated evening before returning to what he had decided would be the ki ing ground.

He thought of the interview with the LAPD people. It had been a monument to Chesterton's bullshitting skills and the economic power of the Consortium—be nice or we'll cancel all your insurance policies, be understanding or nothing in the city government will be underwritten against loss, liability or damage.

He turned off the main road and headed out toward the beach. He wanted someplace deserted, empty of innocent bystanders. Because of the Consortium's influence and some of Track's own, he had gotten his guns back from the police. The SPAS-12 was under his raincoat on the seat beside him, the Randall .45 lying beside it.

There was little traffic at this time in the morning, and Track paced himself to reach Zuma Beach, just north of Malibu, in less than an hour. Twice he saw the oddly reassuring lights in the mirror of the Mercedes.

He wondered how many there would be.

Track checked his watch. It wasn't long until dawn. It was a shame he was on the West Coast rather than the East Coast—dawn was spectacular viewed over the water.

He kept driving. He could feel the butt of the Trapper Scorpion bite into his right side, and he

shifted the Alessi inside-the-pants holster just a little to restore his comfort.

With all four of the men who attacked the printing plant dead, it was imperative that he get one of
the men following him alive.

He eased off the gas pedal and let the Mercedes
slow down, putting it into a parking spot. Shutting
off the ignition, he took the raincoat from the
front seat and stepped out of the car. He picked
up the SPAS-12 and slung it across his body, then
put on the raincoat. He shoved the Randall .45 in
his trouser band, under his vest, then opened his
collar as he pulled his tie down to half mast. The
night was becoming warm.

He locked the car and started walking toward
the sea.

The pockets of the raincoat were weighted down
with shells for the SPAS-12 and the pockets of his
suit coat similarly loaded down with speedloaders
for the L-Frame beneath his shoulder and Detonics 8-round magazines that would work in both
the Randall and the Trapper .45.

He could hear the surf, and saw a hot-dog
stand, closed, shuttered tight.

He heard the automobile-engine sounds behind
him and looked back easily. The now-familiar set
of headlights was positioned beside the Mercedes.
He was half tempted to wave, but he kept walking.

No fires burned along the beach. There was no
evidence of innocent bystanders.

Track stopped. Taking one of the Cuesta-Rey Six-Ts from his case, he guillotined the tip. He settled the cigar between his teeth, biting on it hard. He looked back toward the headlights—the brights came on. The vehicle was starting over the curb and toward the beach, slowly. Track stood waiting for his moment to arrive.

The car was on the sand now, picking up speed, churning the sand in rooster tails in its wake, coming fast now.

Track slung the riot shotgun forward, working the safety in the trigger guard forward. Then his trigger finger snapped back, the SPAS-12 rocking in his hands again and again. One of the headlights was out. The windshield shattered. The thing was still coming. One hundred fifty yards. One hundred yards. Six rounds remained in the SPAS, and gunfire was coming at him from the rear seat of the vehicle—automatic-weapons fire.

Track stood his ground. The SPAS, its stock folded forward over the receiver, was locked tight against his right hip.

He swung his body on line with the automobile's radiator and fired—one Super Slug, then a second, a third, a fourth, a fifth, a sixth. The car skidded and stopped, the hood bursting upward, the radiator spewing like a geyser.

He started to run as the four doors of the car started opening. Men with submachine guns were running on the sand, shouting curses and threats, firing their weapons.

Track was into a dead run along the beach. The surf was a hundred yards to his right, and he loaded the SPAS as he ran. Gunfire plowed the sand around him.

He had the magazine tube half loaded, worked the bolt and pushed the safety forward and swung the SPAS behind him—no slug loads this time, but two-and-three-quarter double O buck. He fired four rounds as fast as he could work the trigger.

Track let the SPAS fall on its sling at his side and he kept running. The gunfire behind him abated slightly, then picked up in volume as Track swung in behind one of the boarded-up hot-dog stands. He held the Trapper Scorpion in one fist and the Randall in the other.

Four men were running along the sand, and he could just make out their Uzis in the growing light. A fifth man was on his knees in the sand, a sixth crouched beside him.

Track fired both .45s at full arm extension, emptying the magazines toward the four running men, tucking back then as subgunfire chewed into the corner of the hot-dog stand.

Track licked his lips and put both empty pistols in his trouser band.

He was feeding double O buck into the magazine tube of the SPAS; eight rounds were loaded.

He worked the magazine cutoff, chambering a ninth round.

He let the SPAS drop on its sling, and reloaded the Trapper Scorpion and the Randall.

He peered around the corner of the hot-dog stand as the automatic-weapons fire stopped.

Two of his attackers were belly-crawling forward like recruits in an infiltration course, their subguns in their upraised hands. Two more had taken shelter behind another of the hot-dog stands. The man who had been on his knees in the sand fifty yards back was lying prone now, and Track could just make out his subgun—down but not out. The fifth man was running a zigzag pattern from the wounded man toward the hot-dog stand.

Track drew the Metalife Custom L-Frame, settling the memory-grooved combat stocks in his right fist. He double-actioned the .357 twice, pumping bullets into the runner's center of mass. A hail of subgunfire poured toward him as the man slammed back into the sand.

Track drew back, and more of the hot-dog stand disintegrated around him as the subgunfire ate away at it.

He plucked the two empties from the cylinder of the L-Frame, freshly loading two single rounds from the dozen or so loose rounds in the vest pockets of his suit.

He holstered it in the X-15 rig.

At the base of the dune, the subgunfire still churning sand about ten yards from him, Track let the SPAS-12 fall to his side on its sling.

He drew the Metalife Custom L-Frame, very slowly raising it, both hands gripping the butt. He took a comfortable point shoulder position, settling the sights about two feet to the right of the subgunner. Track thumbcocked the rounded target hammer and tripped the trigger. A tiny geyser of sand erupted at the subgunner's side. Track shifted the L-Frame to his left, and again he thumbcocked and fired. Another geyser of sand rose and fell to the subgunner's right.

The man had stopped shooting, and Track swung the pistol on line with the man's head. "Your move, amigo!" he shouted.

The subgunner didn't answer.

Track thumbcocked the hammer and stood motionless.

"Wait!" the man shouted. He threw his subgun into the sand about five yards ahead of where he lay.

Track shouted, "Who hired you?"

"I dunno, man. Geez—"

"Who hired you?" Track repeated.

"Look, man, we can make a deal, huh?"

"Only one deal. You tell me and you might live."

His adversary didn't take much time to think it over. "Guy by the name of Stone Hudson—works

He tensioned the SPAS on its sling in a one-handed firing position, and with the Trapper Scorpion in his left fist, Track waited for the automatic-weapons fire to die.

He stepped from behind the corner of the hot-dog stand and fired the SPAS toward the two men belly-crawling across the sand. One of them screamed and was still.

Track swung the Trapper Scorpion toward the hot-dog stand behind which the other two had taken cover. He could see one man's arm and he fired. There was a burst of automatic-weapons fire that drowned out a curse. But Track was already running, firing the SPAS-12 behind him. There was a dune ahead, and as he ran for it something tore at his left leg and he stumbled. He was in pain, and he fired the SPAS as he rolled onto his back. One of the men from the hot-dog stand went down, while the second man, his subgun in his left hand, his right arm dangling at his side, threw himself to the sand.

Track fired again, emptying the SPAS. The Scorpion still had one round left, and he fired it as he painfully stood up. He'd taken a shot in the left thigh, and he favored his left leg as he started up the dune, throwing himself over the top as subgunfire plowed the sand around him. He rolled to the bottom, his mouth filled with sand.

He started to crawl back up to the ridge of the dune.

Reaching the ridge line, he reloaded the Trapper and then laid both .45s on the sand beside him. He peered cautiously over the top. The men were nowhere in sight.

He rolled onto his back for a moment, and taking out a knife, he slit the seam of his trouser leg.

Blood was oozing from a wound in the fleshy part of his left thigh, but the bullet had passed right though. The exit wound was a ragged gash about two inches long. "Fuckin' wonderful," Track rasped.

Looking back over the ridge as he propped up for a second on his elbow he saw that his friends were quiet. "Gimme a minute, guys, and I'll be out to play again," he muttered as he pulled off his shoe and sock.

He reached into his hip pocket for the handkerchief, and folded it to match the size of the wound, getting as much thickness as possible. Then he positioned the handkerchief over the exit wound and tied it down with the sock.

Track stuffed his foot back into his shoe and took another look over the dune.

The three men were apparently still behind the hot-dog stand, and Track decided to undertake a small demolition project. He swung the SPAS up and loaded it with Super Slugs. He settled the sights of the SPAS on the hot-dog stand. "Goodbye, assholes," Track whispered. He touched his finger to the trigger, firing again and again. The

hot-dog stand's walls shattered and Within seconds, the wooden building collapse. One of the subgunners was nothing much left of his head.

A second man broke into a run, and him go. He emptied the SPAS into th hot-dog stand, and the other subgu through a hole in the wall facedown in th

Then Track picked up the Trapper and settled it in both fists. He squinted h the rear sight and whispered "Goodbye fired once, then again. The 185-grain JHP man in the small of the back; his hands fl ward, then grasped for the spine. Th flopped into the sand, twitching for an i then lay still.

Track shoved the Scorpion into his be safety upped. He picked up the Randall ar the same.

Using the butt of the SPAS like a crutch, h himself to his feet.

The last man, the first one wounded, starte ing his subgun, churning sand about twenty y ahead of Track's position at the ridge of the du

Slowly—he had plenty of time, he reasoned— hauled the SPAS up, his weight on his right He started feeding buckshot in the SPAS. Cha bering the ninth round, the safety off, Tra started forward, slowly, his left leg screaming pain.

for some guy based out of the Midwest. Shit, man, that's all I know!" The man rolled, his hands moving. Track waited, seeing the man come up with a pistol in his hand.

The man fired and the sand twenty-five yards in front of Track's feet churned once.

Then the man lay still, his pistol in both hands. "Please, man," he pleaded.

"You lose," Track told him. Then he fired the L-Frame .357 and the man slumped into the sand. Track started walking slowly back to his car. If the cops hadn't heard the racket by now, they weren't going to. The sun was rising over the parking lot where he'd left the Mercedes. "How romantic," he muttered.

28

Molding the plastique was important, and he wanted to pack it just densely enough for a nice clean and uniform ignition. He liked the part—had always liked the part—when one warmed the explosives with the hands. It was a good feeling. There was something very sensual about it.

He did that now, longer than he had to. But it was important, after all, and he felt that he was becoming a part of the latent power that the explosive held.

Making a bomb was a simpler job than this Master of D.E.A.T.H. fellow believed it to be. Timers and hidden timers. The NASA people were so precise in what they did that a timer was excellent.

And to destroy two aircraft the size of yachts was really more or less child's play.

But he had never blown up anything in a weightless environment and he regretted that he would be denied the pleasure of watching it, of learning from it.

One spacecraft would get perilously close to the other.

But the vacuum would be the perfect medium.

No air resistance to slow down the thousands of projectiles that would launch in all directions after the initial explosion.

Thousands of holes would appear in the hull of the second ship. Even a few would do in the right places.

But there would be thousands.

It was, the more he thought about it, an artistic achievement, really.

He had blown up trains, synagogues, public buildings, department stores, buses, houses, cars and aircraft. But never two aircraft at once, let alone spacecraft. That would be interesting. And, of course, never in a vacuum.

And the value of what he was destroying impressed him. He had no idea of the actual unit cost of a space-shuttle orbiter, but it would be in the tens of millions certainly. And each of the three real satellites and this fake one that he was preparing were valued in excess of two hundred million dollars.

He worked the figures in his head. Eight hundred million for the four satellites.

Say another two hundred million for the two shuttle craft—and that was probably conservative, considering all the computer gadgetry and things involved with them.

A billion dollars.

He found himself still warming his plastique.

Klaus Gurnheim smiled. "A billion-dollar bomb. There's a nice ring to it."

29

Two weeks had passed since she had been shot, and he had come to be with her every day since.

His uncle was in Florida, helping Sir Abner Chesterton with the Consortium's end of security for the multiple launch. Zulu had returned safely from Southeast Asia, and through Desiree Goth's underworld contacts was searching for the whereabouts of Stone Hudson—some crazy mercenary colonel, Track had told him.

George smiled at Ellen in her bed. "So how's that sweater you're making me coming along?"

"Fine, George. When do you think they'll let me out of here?"

"They're doing more tests."

"I still can't feel anything below my belly button, George."

"I love you," George told her.

"I know you do." She smiled at him and put her knitting down in her lap. He watched her eyes. "I don't want you coming to see me again. I'll mail you the sweater," she said quietly.

"What the hell are you talking about?"

"How old are you, George?" she asked.

"You know how old I am."

"And that's too young to get yourself stuck with me. I have no feeling, George—no feeling below my belly button, George."

"I don't care about that."

"You will. Leave me now."

"No."

"What do I have to do, George? I'm crippled. You could make love to me until you were raw from it and I wouldn't feel it. Get out of my life," she whispered.

"No."

"George, no girl could ask for anyone nicer, more caring, more faithful. But that won't last. All I'll do is destroy you, or make you destroy yourself. Leave me now," Ellen said.

George Beegh stood up and walked to the bed. He sat on the edge of it and took her hands in his. "You talked about no feeling—beneath your belly button." He smiled at her, watching her brown eyes, and felt that she was suppressing a smile.

"Ohh, George—"

"Hey, let me finish. So you can't walk. Okay, I'll get you the flashiest wheelchair they ever made. As for sex, we can still have a baby. Dr. Freeman told me that. I mean, if you want one. But that's not why I love you, you know. I mean..." George felt embarrassed. "Well, there've been a lot of girls, but there's more to loving somebody than just that. And, anyway, I'm confident—" he laughed "—if anybody can restore feeling down there, hell, old George here can." He kissed both her hands very suddenly, and she rested her forehead against his head as he leaned toward her.

"George, you're incorrigible. But I know—"

"What do you know?" he asked.

"I know you feel this way now, and you're trying to be loyal to me. I really love that about you, George. I mean, nobody could ask for a better friend and everything, but—"

"Hey, you blame me for what happened?" he asked her, his voice low.

"No. Of course I don't blame you. You didn't know those men were going to come and try to kill you. I mean, it could have happened to one of those millions of other girls." She punched him gently in the chest and smiled. "But you're feeling pity for me. That's the only—"

"Shut up," George told her quickly, softly. "You think the only person feeling pity around here is you. Okay, you can't walk. Your life's ruined. May as well ruin it all the way, huh? Bullshit. You go ahead and ruin your own life—don't give a damn about ruining mine. I love you. I want to marry you, be with you."

George folded his arms around her shoulders and drew her to him. His hand brushed against her breast and she giggled. "That tickles."

"Got feeling there, I see?" He smiled, holding her. "How about here?" He brushed his lips against her ear.

"Stop that, George—"

"What about over here?" He crushed his mouth down against hers, kissing her, holding her so tightly that he would never let her go.

30

She thought about Dan Track. If she'd had any
brains she would have married him—she could
have forced it. She thrust her hands into the front
patch pockets of her sundress and continued walking. It was one of those days when her husband's
ancestral estate bored her, and was cold and lonely
despite the warmth of the weather and the warmth
of the sun on her bare shoulders and bare arms.
Pris kicked off her shoes, sinking on her heels into
the grass. She had the gardener and his staff leave
the grass longer out here away from the house.
She wiggled her bare toes in the grass and liked it.

Holding her shoes by the slings in one hand, she
pushed her hair back against the wind as she
walked, the wind outlining her legs beneath her
dress, occasionally billowing up under it. It was a
good feeling.

Free of the house. Free of him.

She considered that. She had been considering it
more and more.

"What would poor Algie do?" she said aloud.
But she knew what he would do. Find some other

rich woman to support him and support his estate. She would wind up getting taken very badly in the divorce—financially. Unless she brought out the information on his affairs.

But that was awfully sordid, she thought, and she had plenty of money, despite Algie's ever-growing collection of Aston-Martins, despite the manor house of Breechmore, which anyone in his right mind would have torn down two centuries ago.

She stopped, watching the pond for a time, feeling the sun hot on her flesh.

It wasn't the cheating—she could tolerate that in a man—it was why *she* cheated, in a desire to be evenhanded and egalitarian. It wasn't the way he spent her money—she had always intended that it be their money. She happened to have the lovely accident of being born rich, whereas Algernon Cole, eleventh earl of Breechmore, had come from a long line of spendthrifts with a reputation to keep up. She imagined he'd been rather inept as a smuggler, too.

He was inept at everything else.

But it was none of that, she thought, the wind dying down, her hand letting go of her hair.

It wasn't meeting Dan Track in France after so many years—she doubted that she could take him away from Desiree Goth. Track didn't care about money at all and besides, Desiree Goth was as rich as she was, perhaps richer.

She dropped to her knees in the grass, putting her shoes down, arranging her skirt around her legs as she sat and watched the stillness of the pond.

Track was an honest man, and she had tired of men who were less than that. And Algie was so much less than that. She didn't really expect Algie or any man to sit down opposite her at the breakfast table and when the servants were out of earshot put down his morning paper, sip his orange juice, light a cigarette, smile and say, "Been cheating on you, darling."

It wasn't that kind of honesty.

Algie had never shared his thoughts with her. Priscilla stood and picked up her shoes. She would go back to the house, take a luxuriant bath, have her maid lay out the new ensemble she had purchased in London the other afternoon, then take herself out to dinner and the theater. Perhaps she would not come home until morning.

Algie wouldn't be back until the next afternoon at any event—and then she would tell him about the divorce.

She started to run across the grassy field. She would miss this place, this field—but nothing else. . . .

SHE HAD LEFT THE THEATER at the end of the second act, driving the XJ-6 with abandon along the country roads, an almost fanatical desire to be alone in her borrowed house for one more night. After she told Algie her need to divorce him—and it was a need, now, a very desperate need to begin again and do it better this time—she would never return to the house again.

In a moment of happiness after her maid had helped her dress, she had told the girl and the other servants to take the rest of the day and the evening off—not to come back until they damned well felt like it, as long as lunch was on the table.

She pulled the Jaguar to a stop in the driveway in front of the house and stepped from the car, searching her beaded bag for her key. She found it as she ascended the steps, but the door, as she discovered when she went to place the key in the lock, was already open.

Her hand froze at the lock.

She had kept the company of men like Dan Track for too many years before marrying Algie not to know what to do. She started back down the steps quickly, dropping the key into her bag.

"Hello, Pris!"

She turned around. "Algie! For Christ's sake, you gave me a start. I thought we had a—"

"A bloody burglar, darling?"

"Yes. How come you're home? You weren't due back from Paris until tomorrow afternoon, I thought."

"Something pressing came up here. Come inside. That's a lovely dress—is it new?"

"Yes," she said, surprised. "Odd you should notice."

"I always notice—I just rarely mention it. Come inside. Pour you a drink, darling Pris?"

"All right," she said as she started back up the steps. "Why aren't there any lights on?"

"I was thinking—sometimes one thinks better in the dark," he called over his shoulder. "Where's your maid? I'm famished. Thought I could get her to make me a sandwich or something."

"I gave her the night off, but I'll make you a sandwich—I still know how."

"You're a dear," he told her.

She hit the switch for the overhead hall light and set her bag down on a small table. Shrugging out of her fur coat, she tossed it onto the chair beside the table.

She turned to face him, but he wasn't there. The lights were on in the library and she walked toward the open doors, assuming he'd gone into the library to make the drinks. She'd have a drink, be a good wife and make his damned sandwich and then tell him she had a "perfectly beastly headache"—he liked it when she sounded British—and go up to bed. Then hope for the best.

She entered the library. Algie's back was to her, and she could hear the tinkle of glasses. "Make mine a double, whatever it is," she sang out, crossing the room in long strides and collapsing onto the couch. She took a cigarette out of the box on the table in front of the couch and lit it. "How was Paris?" she asked.

"Paris is always Paris, isn't it, darling?"

"Pittsburgh's always Pittsburgh—unless they changed the name recently. You know what I mean."

"I did a lot of thinking while in Paris." His back was still turned to her.

Hell, she thought. This was going to start it. "I did some thinking, too, Algie."

"Fortunate for your maid you gave her the night off, Pris darling."

"Why?"

He turned around, staring at her. He was holding a gun.

"What the hell are you . . ." she began.

"Fortunate for your maid because otherwise she would have died, as well," Algie said evenly.

"As well?"

"You don't like me anymore, Pris, and I can't risk your walking away."

"You bastard! You're going to—"

"Kill you and inherit your money? Yes, now you've caught the spirit of the thing, Pris darling."

"You'll never—" She dropped her cigarette.

"Get away with it? I'm in Paris, darling, and have the witnesses to prove it. My old smuggling days stood me in good stead—I crossed the channel, and I'll get back across. I'll be back in Paris in time to be awakened from a very sound sleep after a ridiculously late meeting and be informed of your tragic death after you interrupted a rather violence-prone house burglar. The ancillary advantage is that I'll also have your jewels, which should bring a quarter million easily, plus the insurance to cover their loss."

"Look, fucker—"

"Are those the last words you wish to say?"

"I don't love you," she whispered, crying.

"At last, Pris, at last we have something in common."

She closed her eyes. It was funny, she thought, that she didn't hear any sound. She could only feel this sudden burning in her chest and abdomen. Perhaps the cigarette had burned her dress. No, it was the—

She tried to remember what it was that he had done.

She tried to open her eyes, but she suddenly seemed unable to.

31

Hudson hated Nazis, and he hated listening to Gurnheim. But the Master had specifically asked him to attend Gurnheim's briefing and so he did.

He sat there now, watching the Master watch Gurnheim and his chalkboard drawings of two things that looked like basketballs. He listened and he hated. But he admired, too.

"It is called the Misme-Chardin effect, or sometimes just the plate effect," Gurnheim said. He reminded Hudson of a university lecturer. Sunlight filtered through venetian blinds, making a pattern on the carpet and wall. "The obvious solution to the problem you have presented me with was to construct cylindrical charges running in the same plane as the ship fuselage. But this was the obvious means and vastly less efficient.

"You will recall that I asked that you have made several hollow plastic spheres roughly the size of an American basketball—"

"Same size as Sputnik when it went up," Hudson interjected.

"How very erudite, Colonel," the Master said, then turned away. "Go on, Herr Gurnheim. You will fill these spheres with plastic explosive?"

Gurnheim actually laughed. "Hardly. A very loud noise, a very large explosion—but quantity and quality are not synonymous." Gurnheim turned to his chalkboard. "As I mentioned a moment ago, the Misme-Chardin effect is sometimes referred to as the plate effect. The plates vary in size according to the task required, but the system is the same. For this particular task, I selected steel disks two inches in diameter, each disk one-half-inch thick. Consider these, if you will, as very heavy pieces of shrapnel. There is a general rule of thumb that approximately two times the weight of the disk is needed at standard atmospheric pressure to propel such a disk at a velocity of approximately thirteen thousand feet per second. Now, in the weightlessness of space, the velocity will be unimpeded by friction from the air as one would normally encounter. The gravity effect is also less; therefore, the velocity will be proportionately greater."

"This would be mounted in the spurious satellite we will supply, I take it?" The Master of D.E.A.T.H. said as he stood and approached the chalkboard. "But what of the second ship?"

"At a distance up to a half mile, the shrapnel will be propelled at a velocity sufficient to shred the second shuttle craft. The cosine distribution

falls off rapidly as distance increases, but even using terrestrially based figures, the effect should be
at the least more than adequate—quite spectacular, I think."

"And you have already begun this work?" the
Master asked.

"We only have a couple of days before the
satellite is to be delivered," Hudson felt obliged to
mention.

"I have tested proportionately smaller versions
of this, and I have a demonstration model in my
laboratory."

"I should very much like to see that," the Master said with a smile.

As Gurnheim moved away from the chalkboard, the Master walked beside him. "Colonel
Hudson, please accompany us," the Master said.

Hudson stood up. People like Gurnheim were
crazy, he thought. He shrugged and followed
them into the corridor. The curtains were drawn
back and sunlight streamed through as they turned
left at the end of a short hall and then went down a
flight of carpeted wooden steps to the basement.
The Master hit the panic lock on a bombproof
door and went through with Gurnheim behind
him. Hudson let the door slam closed after him.

On the other side were another flight of steps,
these concrete, and the Master took them at an
easy, familiar clip, Gurnheim plodding after him.
Hudson shook his head.

As they reached the base of the steps, the Master walked ahead along a narrow concrete corridor, stopping before another bombproof door.

Gurnheim approached the door and took a key from his pocket, inserted it into the lock and swung the door open. He stepped inside, the Master behind him. Hudson scanned the corridor in both directions, then nudged his elbow against the Beretta 92SB in the shoulder holster under his left arm and followed inside.

The laboratory was lit by overhead fluorescent fixtures, and the room was bathed in a brilliant, revealing light.

Gurnheim walked past the central worktable to a large cylinder at the far end of the workshop that consumed half of the area of the subbasement.

"I have had this demonstration prepared in expectation of your interest," Gurnheim announced.

Hudson couldn't resist—he peered through a glass porthole at the near end of the huge cylinder.

"The glass," Gurnheim said, "is several layers and several inches thick, but it will allow satisfactory viewing of the demonstration."

Hudson could see two models of space-shuttle craft, the kind children might buy at a model shop for home assembly. They were about three feet apart.

"The distance is relative to the size of these models and the charge has been calculated accordingly. The actual device aboard the first craft will utilize a system of timers and false detonators that cannot be removed or altered without triggering the explosion—it will be tamperproof. For the purposes of this demonstration, I am using radio detonation—this little button.''

Hudson looked away from the toy spaceships and to a gray metal panel about six inches square. Gurnheim flipped up a protective cover, tripped a toggle switch and left his hand poised over a button.

''If you're ready,'' Gurnheim said, ''we will begin.''

Hudson stepped to the right, to allow the Master the viewing port.

''There is room for both of us, Colonel,'' the Master said.

''Yes, sir,'' Hudson responded.

''Herr Gurnheim,'' the Master said evenly, ''you may push the button.''

Hudson stared. The first space shuttle, the one to his right, vaporized in a flash of light to the accompaniment of loud pings emanating from all over the surface of the tank.

The second shuttle model was shredded, and pieces of it littered the base of the cylinder.

''Herr Gurnheim, you are without peer,'' the Master announced. ''Build it at once.''

''I have already begun, sir,'' Gurnheim answered the Master.

"I will not detain you from your labor's completion, Herr Gurnheim. Colonel, come with me, please."

Hudson took one last look inside the cylinder. If it worked like that on the real thing, it would be devastating. He looked at Gurnheim and walked past the Nazi, following the Master out of the laboratory and into the corridor. The Master waited for him. "What is it, sir?" Hudson asked.

"I was terribly disappointed that the attack on the newspaper failed so dismally. And that the men you sent to deal with Major Track failed, as well. In the two and one-half weeks since that story broke, that black freshman congressman Miles Jefferson has instituted a congressional investigation into the existence of our organization. He has gotten nowhere so far."

"I could have gone after Track bastard myself—"

"I know. That is why I have not spoken to you more harshly regarding the failures of your men."

"He's in Florida all the time these days with his damned security deal for the Consortium—I can get him anytime you want."

"That may prove unnecessary. There is no way of tracing me to the manufacturers of the satellite that Herr Gurnheim's little toy will replace. No way, that is, if the president of Argus Communications dies. I want you to see to that immediately after the launch of the first craft. Leave a suicide note, preferably in his own hand, that announces exactly who made the weapon substituted for the real satellite. And that it will go off unless someone who is experienced with Herr Gurnheim's little toys dismantles it. Make it sound as though the president of Argus Communications suffered pangs of conscience. Be creative."

"Why tell them about it, sir?"

"Very simple. They cannot land the craft to dismantle it. They have a second shuttle all ready to go up. They will do the only thing they can do—launch the second craft to rescue the first crew. There will be no time, if we time the release of the note correctly, to remove the satellites from the second shuttle. I have told you of the affair of this Nazi madman named Krieger whom Gurnheim lately served, and I have told you of the part played in it by Major Track. Let me ask you, Colonel, if you were the President of the United States, who would you ask to go up as a mission specialist on the second shuttle craft?"

Hudson, his voice low, answered, "Track."

"Precisely, Colonel. Track will heroically attempt to defuse Herr Gurnheim's bomb. He will be unable to do so and when the bomb detonates, not only will there be the greatest single insurance loss in the history of the world, which will destroy my enemy the Consortium, but we shall have eliminated Major Track, as well."

"I gotta hand it to you, sir, that's—"

The Master of D.E.A.T.H. stopped at the base of the concrete steps, turned, smiled and supplied a word. "Diabolical?"

32

Dan Track, Sir Abner Chesterton and Desiree Goth had been eating lunch in the pleasant town of Titusville, Florida. The seat of Brevard County, it was founded in 1867 by Colonel Henry T. Titus as Sand Point. In 1874 it was renamed in his honor. In the beginning, Titusville was served by a mule-drawn railway that carried freight thirty-five miles inland. It was now served by the world's first space port, a place for carrying freight thousands of miles upward. In 1960, the population was slightly less than six thousand five hundred. By 1970, the population of Titusville was nearly five times that.

Dan Track had been having a hamburger and French fries, Sir Abner Chesterton a BLT and Desiree Goth a cold turkey sandwich.

It was then that the man Track and Chesterton had worked with prior to the launch of the first shuttle craft walked into the restaurant. With him was an Air Force general Track didn't recognize and an FBI agent Track did recognize. The man from Cape Kennedy was Thomas Martin, number-two man in security. The general, Track learned from his name tag, was Brolton. The FBI agent was Benjamin Hask.

When the three men had approached the table, Track had looked up. "Hi, guys," he'd said.

Thomas Martin had not smiled. He had handed over a piece of paper, a laser photo facsimile of a handwritten suicide note. After taking a look at it, Track passed it to Sir Abner. As he rose from the table, Track said to General Brolton, "Pay the bill, would you, sir?"

THERE HAD BEEN NO TIME for any training.

After the twenty minutes spent on the telephone to the President in the Oval Office, Track had been fitted with a space suit. Then he asked for five minutes, telling them to delay the countdown if they had to, and he had found a room alone with Desiree Goth.

"You're not an astronaut. You're not a demolitions expert."

"I know Klaus Gurnheim's bombs better than any man alive."

"You'll be killed.'

"I won't be killed—at least I hope not."

"Dan—"

"I know."

"I love you."

"I know that, too." It was then she had cried. . . .

DESIREE GOTH WATCHED, Sir Abner Chesterton's arm around her shoulder. The launch was like a pillar of fire. "He won't come back, Abner."

"He'll come back, Desiree. If anyone can, Dan will come back."

"If he does," she whispered, watching the diminishing shape of the phallus-shaped spacecraft in the sky downrange from the launchpad, "we're going to be done with this. All of it. He wants that, too. He asked me to marry him."

"Congratulations, my dear. Even under the circumstances, that is fine news."

She leaned her head against Sir Abner's chest, and felt his arm tighten around her.

"He'll be the one who does it, I know that. Dan won't let someone else take the chance."

"That's the sort of person he is," she heard Chesterton telling her, feeling his voice reverberate in his chest.

"Give me your handkerchief." She sniffed.

She felt him pressing it into her hand. He was talking again. "If—when, I mean—Dan returns, he'll go after the Master. He'll have to."

"I know."

"We can find you both a place—far away. Where you can renew yourselves."

"Yes, far away from everything."

He placed his hands on her upper arms and she felt him turning her around gently, slowly. She looked up into his soft blue eyes. "After you've

both had a long time away, we'll all get together—
one last time—all of us. We'll tear George away
from Ellen to help. We'll formulate a plan that
will eliminate the Master of D.E.A.T.H. and
destroy his organization.'' And he smiled more
broadly. ''And then I'll return to London and go
to my club a great deal, George and Ellen will put
their lives together, you'll turn over running your
business to Zulu and you and Dan will be on your
own. And I'll hear from you at Christmas, and
when there are birth announcements. You'll come
to London, and we'll sit around and drink horribly expensive champagne. Your children will call
me Uncle Abner, and we'll laugh about the dan-
gers we all endured together.''

''Will it be that way?'' she asked.

''It will be that way,'' he said. ''It has to be.''

''CONTROL—THIS IS RESCUE ONE. We are single-
engine press to MECO—I repeat—single-engine
press to MECO, over.''

''Roger, Rescue One, we copy. Looking good
here as well. Out.''

Captain Phillip O'Toole looked away from his
console. ''Well, Major Track, what do you think
of space flight?''

Dan Track looked at the commander's panel.
''It's different,'' he said.

But already O'Toole was looking away. Track
could hear the voice from Ground Control. ''Res-

cue, this is Control. Main engine throttle down.''

"Roger on that. Out."

The pilot, Captain Billings, a pretty red-haired woman, said, "Major Track, if you're wondering what we're doing, well, we're keeping our acceleration to less than three Gs. In another minute or so we'll have throttled down to sixty-five percent of thrust. That's what MECO meant a minute back—Main Engine Cutoff."

Track smiled. "Is it too late to get Scotty to beam me down?" he asked.

Captain Billings laughed. "Going up's the easy part."

"I was afraid you were going to say that. Can't smoke a cigar, I suppose?"

She laughed again.

The voice of Ground Control cut in again. "Rescue, this is Control. Go for Main Engine Cutoff. Over."

"Main Engine Cutoff on schedule. Got ourselves a nervous passenger here," O'Toole said. "But he's hanging in there, over."

"Rescue, this is Control. We copy that. Got a few nervous people on the ground here, too. Over."

O'Toole laughed. "Ground, this is Rescue. I've got three red Main Engine Status Indicators. Once they blink out we're going for E.T."

Track shook his head. "E.T.?"

O'Toole laughed. "Sorry to disappoint you. We're not phoning home, just going for External Tank separation."

"Ohh."

33

When he was a kid, he had ridden on a train once that wasn't fitted with chemical toilets. You flushed and looked down inside and you could see the rails speeding away beneath you. Before Track used the WCS, Captain Billings had explained how it worked.

"It's really kind of cute. Open the door and extend the privacy curtains. Here's your operating handle and control panel. When the handle's forward, the gate valve opens."

"WCS?"

"Waste Collection System. The toilet uses air instead of water. There are blades that rotate—we call it a slinger—and shred the stool and sort of spray paints it on the interior walls of the pot. Okay?"

"Wonderful."

"When you put the handle in the off position, the vent valve opens and exposes the pot to the vacuum of space. That dries the—"

"The shit?"

"Yes, if you want to say it that way."

"What happens if you push the handle the wrong way when you're sitting on it? I mean, would you get—"

"I don't think so," she said with a smile.

"Good." But the idea of being adrift in space haunted him....

THE FIRST SHUTTLE, designated Orbit One for the mission, had placed itself into orbit more miles up than Track wanted to consider. Rescue One had moved into position some three hundred yards behind it and slightly above it in order to view at an oblique angle the open cargo bay and the gleaming satellite and rocket booster called Link-Com III. The remote manipulator arm had already been moved partially into place. Captain Billings, standing to Track's left as the aft crew station on one of the variable height platforms, said, "They were afraid to do anything with the arm, anything at all. What if the payload-assist module was rigged to go off—"

"That's what you call the rocket booster that would have put the little sucker into orbit?"

"Yes, that's what we call the rocket booster that would have put the little sucker into orbit, Major."

"All right, I don't think it's in the payload-assist module. Otherwise NASA security people would have detected something wrong. It's in the guts of the satellite itself. Link-Com III is the bomb.'' Track pushed his hands into the cobalt blue slacks of his space gear and stared out the open port. "So we can't move it without possibly triggering it—that's what they figured. Well, they're wrong. It'll have a time detonator, and we've probably got several hours on that yet. You guys got up here earlier than planned. Gurnheim would have wanted both shuttles together, get both at once.''

"A bomb that powerful?"

Track looked at the female pilot. "Power and effectiveness can sometimes be mutually exclusive. I'd say he'll be going for a Misme-Chardin effect.''

"A what me what?"

Track laughed. "He's probably got steel plates the size of half-dollars backed up by plastic explosives. When the thing goes off, however he constructed it, whether cylindrically or spherically, the plastique will blow Orbit One to bits, and the plastique will launch the little steel plates either in vectors roughly approximating an X-shape or if he used a sphere as the basis, then in an ever-widening pattern.''

"I don't understand.''

"Ever fire a shotgun?"

"Yeah, sure I have. My dad used to take me dove shooting.''

"Fine,'' Track told her. "Imagine the disks in the Misme-Chardin effect being like a shot column—the closer the object struck, the tighter the column and the tighter the pattern. The farther away, conversely. Okay?''

"Then you'll have to be very careful when you dismantle it."

"I can't dismantle it," Track told her. "If Klaus Gurnheim built it, he'll have built it so it cannot be dismantled without being set off. And doubtless he'll have backed it up with some sort of system that would cause it to detonate if the... what did you call it?"

"The payload-assist module?" she supplied.

"Yes, if the payload-assist module is set into operation. The funny thing with Gurnheim is that he does it for the challenge, I think. Which is why he's the most dangerous bomb man there is. He would have left some way that is almost impossible to figure out, even more impossible to effect, but some way it could be disarmed. It's a game between him and whoever tries to deactivate the bomb. He did one once that was a nuclear weapon set up like a video game. A young kid played out the video game against Gurnheim's program. Beat the game.''

"A video game?"

Track laughed. "The funny thing, after the boy beat the game, after the bomb was disarmed, the kid wanted to know where he could get the game so he could play it at home."

Captain Billings laughed. But after a moment,

she spoke softly, saying, "What are you going to do?"

"I'm going to put on that crazy space suit they issued me and go out after it. By the time I get over to the other shuttle, you and Captain O'Toole will have gotten the crew of Orbit One safely aboard this craft. I'll start to work after you guys have withdrawn."

"We can't withdraw, like you say," Captain Billings told him. "We didn't finish the final fueling process—that's why we were able to take off earlier and buy the extra time. We have a safe amount of fuel to deorbit and start reentry. Once the Rescue One pulls away from Orbit One, well, there's no coming back."

Track closed his eyes. "All right." And he laughed. "If this were a movie, I'd just slide over there and disarm the bomb, then get on the radio and have them talk me down. I even fly fixed wing and helicopter. Should be a snap—if it were a movie."

"Even if you were qualified, it wouldn't be the easiest thing to land one of these yourself."

"You ever land one?" Track asked her, smiling.

"On simulator, hundreds of times." She smiled. "This is my first time up as pilot."

Track started to say something, but she cut him off. "O'Toole will have the crew of Orbit One aboard. He won't need me. One of these flies just like another. Orbit One's pilot can land Rescue One. I'll land Orbit One."

"Bullshit," Track told her.

"Ever use a backpack for maneuvering—an MMU?"

"Manned Maneuvering Unit, right?" Track asked with a smile. "No, I haven't."

"I've practiced with it, as much as you can without using it here. You can't go alone. And what if you need an extra pair of hands, Major?"

"I'll grow them," Track told her. "Look, Captain—you go out there with me, fine. Maybe it increases our chances for success, but it pretty much signs your death warrant. The chances aren't that great to begin with."

"My mother asked me why I became an astronaut. I'll tell you the same thing I told her. I was one of the first female test pilots. No woman had flown one of these things, and I didn't know if I'd be the first but I knew for damn sure I wouldn't be the last. You want opportunity in this life, Major, you take some chances. And if that bomb does go off, maybe Rescue One won't be far enough away, shrapnel will travel for miles up here. There are Soviet satellites above us. What if one of those gets destroyed? The possibilities are endless, aren't they? And you can't let some bastard like this Master of D.E.A.T.H. guy you've been talking about play with human lives, or some crazy man like this Gurnheim blow things up that people have sweated blood to build.''

Track stuck out his hand and she took it. He asked her, "If we get out of this, is it okay to kiss a fearless test pilot?"

"Only if she lets you," Captain Billings said with a smile.

Captain Billings had gotten into her EVA suit in five minutes. It had taken Track seven minutes with her helping to set the connections to the liquid cooling and ventilation undergarment, get the Snoopy hat in place with his radio headset and finally fit the helmet. He had been in the dependent mode of pure-oxygen breathing for the prescribed two hours and felt light-headed.

The air lock was set for use on a Spacelab Transfer Tunnel, and she had checked the air lock's life-support system, then sealed the hatch.

He heard her voice coming through the earmuffs. "I'm adjusting the knob on your suit to the EVA position."

"Wonderful," Track told her, miles past bafflement.

"You're sure you understand the controls for the MMU?"

Track nodded, the helmet feeling awkward to him. "The right hand controls pitch, roll and yaw. And the left grip controls straight-line movement."

"Don't try anything too fast or fancy. The supply of nitrogen gas isn't infinite and you could launch yourself into orbit with this if you screwed up badly enough."

"Go ahead," Track said, "build up my confidence."

"Just do what I do, nice and slowly. We're leaving now."

Track nodded.

"Keep your visor down," she was telling him as she opened the exterior air-lock door. "Tell me if the LEDs on your chest-mounted microcomputer start showing any of those things I warned you about."

"Yes, ma'am."

"Fine. We're going to walk into the cargo bay now."

"I hate this," Track said.

"Good. Remember that and do what I tell you to," she cautioned. She was through, Track moving after her. Suddenly he was free floating. "Track! Wake up!"

"What?"

"Don't be so awed by it that you die."

"Sorry."

"Correct your pitch—up about fifteen degrees."

"Which way is up?"

"Toward me, okay?"

"Okay, kid." Track worked his right-hand controls. He overshot the mark and started spinning, but closed his eyes for an instant, correcting a little at a time, feeling like a first-time driver learning on a Ferrari.

She was beside him, helping him. "You're doing too much. Go slow, okay?"

"Right."

He looked around him. Even through the visor, the beauty was there, the emptiness of it was overwhelming, but there was something beautiful about that, too. "I tell you—" He realized from the sound of his own voice that he needed to control his breathing. "I tell you, Captain, this is the most beautiful place I've ever died in."

"Don't say that."

"Avoiding saying something doesn't change it," he told her. The three hundred yards to Orbit One were a very long three hundred yards—it looked more like three hundred miles. He could see its open cargo bay clearly, and Link-Com III seemed to stare back at him. It was waiting to kill him.

"Right behind you," Track said. "Take it easy for us first-time drivers."

"Better believe I will, Major."

"It's Dan, Captain Billings."

"Elizabeth."

"Elizabeth—pretty name for an astronaut."

"Dan's a pretty name for an insurance investigator and counterterrorist."

"Touché," Track said, working his MMU's left control and propelling himself forward.

Track could hear the commander's voice. "This is O'Toole. We've got everybody aboard through the aft crew station air lock. We'll be getting under way for deorbit in about another eighteen minutes. Should be time for you both to assess the situation and see about returning here."

"We won't be coming back, O'Toole," Elizabeth Billings's voice said through his headset.

"Look, Liz, no sense getting yourselves killed."

"She's right," Track said into his microphone. "We've got to defuse the bomb if we can. Can't abandon Orbit One. Can't let the bastards who did this win."

Track had cut the distance to the Orbit One cargo bay by more than two-thirds, and remembering her instructions, he started to slow and position himself. Elizabeth Billings was there ahead of him, starting toward Link-Com III. "Don't touch the damn thing," Track said to her.

"Wouldn't dream of it, Dan. Take your time."

"Wouldn't have it any other way." He was trying to keep the talk light, and he realized why. He was scared to death. But not by death. Or by D.E.A.T.H.

He was nearly into position, and Elizabeth seemed to be kneeling beside the satellite.

It was cylindrically shaped and shone as though it were covered with burnished gold. The payload-assist module looked like a conventional rocket engine of the type seen in museums.

He hooked himself into place beside the Link-Com III.

"What now?" Elizabeth Billings's voice came back.

"We fake it, Liz, we fake it. Is this an access hatch into the guts of the satellite?"

"No! That's a solar panel covering that opens automatically after the payload has been elevated to its final orbit." She was silent for a moment, looking at the thing, he guessed. "There's the access hatch. According to the diagrams they gave us before we took off, about two inches below this there could be room for one of the charges you talked about."

Track was still staring at the satellite. "I'm betting a spherical charge. What the hell are these?" He gestured toward something that looked like a massive, futuristic smoke alarm.

"That's the spin table."

"How the hell do these things work?"

"What—launching a satellite?"

"Yeah," Track told her, gently touching the framework beneath the satellite.

"Okay, everything's held in the cradle here, beneath the satellite. The base of the payload-assist module is locked into this. Electric motors, in this thing—" she pointed to the object Track had thought looked like a huge smoke alarm "—start to spin the entire assembly on its axis. After the assembly is released from the cradle, the spin continues, obviating any problems with the thrust of the PAM being out of balance. It continues to spin until the PAM fires, then—''

''Wait a minute! I know what he did this time,'' Track whispered into his microphone. ''I know what he did—it's the only thing he could have done. Son of a bitch.''

''What do you mean? What are you—''

''All right. He would have set this thing up with hidden detonators, trip detonators, every single thing he could have done to prevent me or anyone else from disarming it. We know that. Yet he wanted a way to prevent anyone from just throwing it out and letting it detonate later. Rigging another detonator to the payload-assist module wouldn't have been possible since the people who made the satellite didn't rig the payload-assist module to it. And, anyway, the thing might have been too far away to have the effect he wanted—''

''It doesn't fire until after forty minutes, after release from the spin table.''

''Perfect,'' Track said, staring at the satellite. ''He would figure we'd think there's something with the PAM, anyway. But to get rid of the thing by firing it off early or—''

''We don't call it firing it off.''

''I don't care,'' Track snapped. ''All right, follow my logic, Liz. The logical thing for us to do would be to release this thing from its cradle and manually take it out to some safe distance, then fly out of here.''

''Agreed.''

''So that's where the booby trap is, in removal of the satellite from the cradle. Somewhere in there there's something magnetic, probably, and the separation—''

''What are you saying? We can't defuse it, can't get rid of it?''

''Can this cradle be removed, torched off—whatever?''

''There are electrical cables.''

''We can cut them. No direct connections to the spin table?''

''No.''

''Then we're all right—maybe. You got a torch in this thing?'' he said, gesturing to the spacecraft.

''Yes, we should—''

''Get it, and anything else that might prove useful—electrical tape and get a rope. Is there another MMU?''

''There should be a spare one for this trip.''

''Bring it, as well. I'll keep an eye on the baby, but make it quick. We still don't know what time the little sucker's set to go off.''

BEFORE ELIZABETH BILLINGS had returned with the torch, the rope and the extra MMU, while Dan Track had been sweating inside his space suit and telling himself he had to have guessed right, the voice of Captain Phillip O'Toole came to him through the earphones in the snoopy hat he wore under his space helmet. "Major—this is O'Toole."

"What is it, Captain?"

"Look, I monitored your communications with Liz—that shuttle is only a piece of equipment. It costs a lot, but it can be replaced."

"Are y u telling me to let the Master of D.E.A.T.H. and Klaus Gurnheim win? Just abandon it?"

"I should be making the burn to start our re-entry, but I can wait until you and Liz make it back."

"You'd be too crowded."

"We've got people strapped to the bulkheads as it is, but we can fit two more. Give it up."

Track watched the satellite gleam as it caught a glow of sunlight over the horizon of the earth below. "You know, I almost envy you guys. Getting to do this sort of thing. It's so pretty."

"Look, Major—"

"No, you look. Let's say this sucker blows up. What happens when all the people who want the space program cancelled because it costs too much start saying, 'See, we told you so' and shit like that? What happens when the Master wins? No, you start your burn, you get your people home."

And then Dan Track heard the voice of Liz Billings—it sounded so close he turned around to look, almost losing his hold on the satellite. But she was still inside Orbit One, he realized. She was talking to O'Toole. "Phil, what Dan said goes double for me. Get your people out of here. Orbit One was abandoned. I'm taking charge as commander. So you get your vehicle on the road—and thanks, O'Toole."

And then he heard the voice of Phillip O'Toole. "I'll be starting the burn. God be with you both."

"And you, too, Captain O'Toole—get them all back safe, huh?"

It seemed like an eternity as he watched the Rescue One turn itself so that it was pointed tail first into its flight path. He watched the engines fire, expecting to hear something—but there was nothing to hear he realized. He had watched too many outer space operas where laser blasts and rocket engines were heard miraculously in the void of space where there was no air to carry sound. He marveled at the silence of it. He felt something touch him and he looked to his right. Liz Billings had returned, laden with the items from Orbit One. He could see the glow of the shuttle craft's rocket engines reflected in the visor of her helmet. Her voice seemed subdued. "He's doing an OMS burn now—orbital maneuvering system. Considering the weight he's got..."

Track didn't listen anymore. "It's a funny feeling, Liz. Watching Rescue One that way. You sort of feel like the guy left behind on the desert island—at least I do.''

"As we work here, you'll see the shuttle sinking away from you. You won't notice it at first. He has to turn the ship around again. But the ship will start to drop. It should look smaller to you, as if you were looking at it through a zoom magnification telescope, but backward, and you kept gradually increasing the power.''

"Are you frightened?" Track whispered.

"What?"

"Are you frightened?" he said again.

"Yes, I think I am.''

"Good," Track said. "I didn't want to think I was the only one. Let me see that torch. Got a match?"

"A match?"

"Just trying to cheer you up—so you can cheer me up.''

IT TOOK THE BETTER PART of two hours to cut away the main joints of the cradle, and Track left one partially cut support on each side to prevent the satellite and its cradle from floating away. He had attached the rope to the cradle and attached that to some of the other security grommets nearby. With the torch he cut away the remaining support on the starboard side. It started to shift, but only slightly.

"You got a knife?"

"Swiss Army knife, but it's not with me."

"We'll use the torch to cut the rope. We need to cut off the loose rope and secure our MMUs to it, then cut away the ropes restraining the cradle. Start getting out of your MMU."

"What about you?" she asked.

"I'll keep mine on and take you back piggyback. That spare one we can attach to the cradle."

"I've got news for you—in space you don't weigh any more than I do. I'll take you back piggyback. I'm not trusting your driving."

"Fair enough," Track told her. He had torched away the other support. He handed her the torch. "Cut the extra rope for us." He began skinning out of the MMU. . . .

HE HELD ON TO HER—there was no rope left for a safety line. And only Liz Billings had an MMU. When he torched the two rope restraints on the cradle, he would have to manipulate the MMU on the starboard side of the cradle, then use the tape she had brought to lock the forward-motion controls. She would lock the control of the MMU on the port side.

Then they would both let go. Rescue One was no longer visible—it would be getting ever closer to landing at Edwards AFB. If this worked, Orbit One would land back at Kennedy.

He took the torch and swung across from her to the port-side MMU and cut the restraining line beneath the cradle. It shifted, almost throwing him. Then he crawled across the top of the satellite and the PAM to the other side of the metal cradle and freed it with the torch. The cradle shifted radically. He let go of the torch, and reached for the MMU controls to get the direction of the improvised launch.

"We're in position," he heard Liz say. "Countdown for setting forward motion—"

"Okay," Track answered.

"At zero. Ten, nine, eight, seven—"

He was sweating inside his suit, and he wondered if he would have the courage to let go and drift free, waiting for her to come to him with her MMU. Otherwise he would drift until his suit ran out of oxygen, or until he froze or boiled.

"Three, two, one—zero!"

The cradle with its MMUs propelling it shot forward and Track let go, his body twisting, spinning in space uncontrollably. With each turn he saw another angle of the space shuttle or the cradle that held the bomb-rigged satellite. He realized he was screaming into his headset. "Liz!"

And suddenly his motion slowed. "I've got you, Dan—hold on to me."

He locked his fists onto her suit; he was like a drowning man.

He could see the satellite in the distance. Soon it would explode.

He could hear Liz telling him, "How about I

give you a ride home. And I'll even let you give me that kiss."

He closed his eyes. "Home sounds good to me." He tried not to think of the fact that if the satellite blew up in the next ten minutes, it would still likely kill them.

34

The bomb had exploded thirteen minutes after they had launched it with the MMUs. Thirteen, he thought—maybe there was something to that number after all.

"This is the rotational hand controller I'm using," Liz Billings said, breaking into his thoughts.

Dan Track realized he was gripping the arm rests of his seat so hard that his fingers were numbing—he looked at his hands and they were white knuckled, the fingertips beneath his fingernails bluish purple. "The what?"

"The RHC. I'm speed breaking to 100 percent—"

"Why aren't we stopping?" Track asked Liz Billings.

"Well, we are stopping really. It's like the old mechanical brakes on sports cars—you just have to keep at it. But I'm pitching our nose forward, now! We've got—" Track felt a bone-shattering jar "—nose wheel touchdown!"

He could hear the ground control voice on the

speaker. "Orbit One—nose wheel at contact. Looking really good."

"Roger, out. Thanks," Liz Billings spoke into the microphone near her lips.

She had pretty lips. After entering Orbit One and removing his helmet, he hadn't waited for her to strip out of her EVA suit. He'd simply told her, "Okay, Liz, I earned that kiss." And she'd given it to him and it had been one hell of a kiss, he thought.

"Speed break full forward," she said suddenly.

"What's that mean?" Track asked her.

"We're on the ground and we're stopped, Dan!" And she looked at him and she smiled, her red hair falling into her eyes as she tossed her head and laughed. She was talking into the microphone, "This is Orbit One to Convoy One— wheels stop, over."

A new voice came over the speaker. "Orbit One, this is Convoy. You are wheels stop, welcome home. Convoy out."

She was flipping switches, and Track had stopped counting at ten.

"It isn't just like shutting off the family car," she said with a laugh. "You want to do the most important thing?"

Track looked at her, a questioning look on his face.

Laughing, she told him, "See that computer keyboard?"

He followed where she pointed her right index finger. "Yeah."

"Unstrap yourself and push the keys I tell you to."

Track nodded, working open his seat restraints and standing—he was surprised that he still could.

"Now," she said as he leaned over her, "I want you to punch the upper case 'O'—" But he leaned farther forward, and kissed her.

"You're a brave lady," he said, "and a pretty one. Thanks for sticking with me out there."

"You were the brave one—" And she raised her hands to his face and pressed her mouth against his.

A voice came over the speaker. "Orbit One, this is Control. We're not getting a reading that you've entered the shut down code into your computer. Confirm please, over?"

Her lips moved to his ear and she whispered, "Desiree Goth is a lucky woman."

As Track pulled back he said, "You give new meaning to the phrase 'friendly skies,' kid."

She looked up at him, and then the voice said again, "Orbit One, are you receiving me?"

There had been no heroes' welcome. No one outside the security people at NASA, the Consortium and those other few with the need to know would ever know. The news media had been told that one of the satellites had been irretrievably lost, not because of a NASA error but rather an error in the construction of the satellite. In a way, that was true.

After a long night of physical exams, debriefings, a congratulatory call from Washington and a night's sleep that had been the end to so much exhaustion that he and Desiree Goth had merely fallen asleep in each other's arms, Dan Track sat near the head of a long conference table. Orange juice, an eight-ounce ribeye cooked medium, hash brown potatoes and two eggs sunny side up and barely warmed were on the table in front of him. The conference-room door opened. It was Captain Phillip O'Toole, the commander of Rescue One, and beside him, wearing a pink sundress and a shawl over her bare shoulders, was Captain Liz Billings. O'Toole walked across the room, a big grin on his face, his right hand behind him.

As O'Toole stopped beside Track's chair, Track stood. "Major," O'Toole said, "how about a beer? I know breakfast isn't quite the time for it, but—" and he shoved his right hand forward. There was a bottle of Michelob in it.

Track took the bottle from him, twisted off the cap and slugged down a quarter of the bottle. And then he laughed. "You're right, breakfast isn't the time for it." And he set down the beer and took O'Toole's right hand and shook it.

He heard the laughter from the opposite side of the table. He looked past Desiree Goth, who was smiling, past Sir Abner Chesterton whose face seemed etched with worry, to Zulu. "What the hell is so funny?" he asked.

"I confess, Major, you are," Zulu said, and he laughed again.

Track sat down opposite Desiree. O'Toole sat at his right, and Liz Billings sat beside Desiree. While he ate he divided his attention between Zulu's updating on the continuing search for the mercenary Stone Hudson and whatever it was Desiree Goth and Liz Billings were laughing about.

Finally, he looked across the table at Chesterton. "Sir Abner, you should be happy. No insurance loss. We messed up the plans of the Master. Desiree and I will be out of your hair for a while—"

Chesterton interrupted. "Well, I am happy, certainly. Dan, you and Captain Billings and Captain O'Toole deserve a hearty cudo from the Consortium for that one. And as to you and Desiree being out of my hair—" and he smoothed his hair with the palm of his right hand "—it's not really that crowded up there, as you can see," and he smiled. But then the smile faded. "But I'm afraid I do have some bad news for you and Desiree—especially you, Dan. I understand you knew Priscilla Cole, the wife of Algernon Cole, the earl of Breechmore?"

Track put down his fork. "What about her?"

"Nasty business, I'm afraid. The earl was away in Paris on business and she had given the household staff the night off. Gone to a play and returned early. She evidently surprised a house burglar, and—''

Track stood up. Something fell to the floor from the table and broke. Everyone was silent, watching him.

Chesterton continued to speak. "I'm sorry, Dan—she was shot to death."

Dan Track closed his eyes. He remembered the look in her eyes when he had as much as accused Breechmore of sending the Trans Am after them that night and trying to kill him. Fear.

His voice low, his eyes still closed, Track said very slowly, "People don't die that coincidentally, do they, Sir Abner?"

"You are implying—"

Track opened his eyes. "Damned right I am."

"I can do some checking, I suppose," Zulu volunteered.

"Priscilla dead," Desiree murmured.

"Priscilla murdered," Dan Track corrected....

TRACK HAD BEEN IN NO RUSH—he had wanted to be sure. After he did it, he would take Desiree away for a time, to rest, to recover his sanity before going after the Master of D.E.A.T.H. one more time. He hoped for good.

Through Desiree's contacts he had checked things the local police near the estate of the eleventh earl of Breechmore could not have checked, things Scotland Yard could not have discovered.

Through her contacts in the French underworld, Track had learned of the boat—the face of the man who had hired it had been the face of Algie Cole. The boat had taken him to England and back.

They were in England, and as they sat in the Mercedes, Track said to Desiree, "After this and after we take that time for ourselves, then we get the Master and Gurnheim and this Colonel Hudson bastard. Then we'll have a real rest. But you understand, I have to do this."

"If you didn't, I would."

"You didn't have to be my wheel man." He smiled, holding her hand against his thigh.

"I wanted to be."

He tried his Humphrey Bogart voice on her. "All right, sweetheart, keep the engine running so we can hightail it out of here if the cops spot us."

"That's not very good."

"I know," he sighed. He leaned over to her and kissed her.

He had arranged an alibi for them both, and it would hold up. He had had Breechmore's movements monitored. All that remained was to get out of the car, walk the few paces to the front door, and when Breechmore opened the door, kill him.

Track opened the door of the Mercedes and stepped out onto the gravel. He walked up the steps to the door.

He knocked, and waited.

The door opened. "Track! I say—" Breechmore said.

"Algie," Track replied coldly.

"Desiree—that her in the Mercedes?"

"Yes."

"I gather you've heard about Pris's death then. It was—"

"Tragic," Track supplied.

"Well, quite—yes. Come in."

"No," Track said. He noticed Algie was looking at his hands. "Why did you kill Pris, Algie?"

"Kill Pris? You're mad, Track."

"I know you killed her, Algie. I've followed your trail."

"Try to prove that," Breechmore said and he began to close the door. Track shoved it violently open, knocking Algie back into the hallway.

"Admit it to me," Track said to him.

"I'll admit nothing. You can't prove what you say. Guilty or not, if you can't prove it, no court of law will convict me."

"You're not even sorry," Track whispered.

"She's dead and I'm glad of it," Breechmore said, taunting him. "Now get out of my house."

"Why?" Track asked.

"Money, dear fellow. Why do you think? She was going to divorce me."

"Why didn't you just shoot her in the head?"

Track asked, his voice soft. "You shot her in the gut. It took her a long time to die."

"I wanted it to look like a robbery, old man, not an assassination."

There was a moment of silence. Then Dan Track drew a Walther P-5 from his trouser band. "I don't care how this looks at all," he said.

He raised his pistol.

"You wouldn't," the eleventh earl of Breechmore said, surly and sure of himself.

Track squeezed the trigger.

MORE GREAT ACTION
COMING SOON

When there's no one else to turn to!

TRACK

#9 THE D.E.A.T.H. HUNTERS
by Jerry Ahern

It's a routine snowstorm in Storm City, Idaho—until the snow becomes a silent killer and bodies start turning up covered in green mold.

At the same time, Dan Track and Desiree Goth are trapped in a chalet perched on an Idaho mountainside when the ski-shack is ripped apart by rocket explosions.

Someone is out to get them—and all of mankind—by staging a biological atrocity that will wipe out the major cities of the world. That someone is the Master of D.E.A.T.H., the evil genius behind the Directorate for Espionage, Assassination, Terrorism and Harassment.

To save his life and those of millions of others, Dan Track must go on a hunt, a D.E.A.T.H. hunt!

Enter the
'Gear Up For Adventure Sweepstakes'
You May Win a 1986 AMC Jeep® CJ
Off-road adventure — Only in a Jeep.®

OFFICIAL RULES
No Purchase Necessary

1) To enter print your name, address and zip code on an Official Entry or on a 3" x 5" piece of paper. Enter as often as you choose but only one entry allowed to each envelope. Entries must be postmarked by January 17, 1986 and received by January 31, 1986. Mail entries first class. In Canada to Gold Eagle Gear Up For Adventure Sweepstakes, Suite 233, 238 Davenport Rd., Toronto, Ontario M5R 1J6. In the United States to Gold Eagle® Gear Up For Adventure Sweepstakes, P.O. Box 797, Cooper Station, New York, New York 10276. Sponsor is not responsible for lost, late, misdirected or illegibile entries or mail. Sweepstakes open to residents 18 years or older at entry of Canada (except Quebec) and the United States. Employees and their immediate families and household of Harlequin Enterprises Limited, their affiliated companies, retailers, distributors, printers, agencies, American Motors Corporation and RONALD SMILEY INC. are excluded. This offer appears in Gold Eagle publications during the sweepstakes program and at participating retailers. All Federal, Provincial, State and local laws apply. Void in Quebec and where prohibited or restricted by law.

2) First Prize awarded is a 1986 Jeep CJ with black soft top and standard equipment. Color and delivery date subject to availability. Vehicle license, driver license, insurance, title fees and taxes are the winner's responsibility. The approximate retail value is $8,500 U.S./$10,625 Canadian. 10 Second Prizes awarded of a Sports Binocular. The approximate retail value is $90 U.S./$112.50 Canadian. 100 Third Prizes awarded of Gold Eagle Sunglasses. The approximate retail value is $6.95 U.S./$8.65 Canadian. No substitution, duplication or cash redemption of prizes. First Prize distributed from U.S.A.

3) Winners will be selected in random drawings from all valid entries under the supervision of RONALD SMILEY INC. an independent judging organization whose decisions are final. Odds of winning depend on total number of entries received. First prize winner will be notified by certified mail and must return an Affidavit of Compliance within 10 days of notification. Winner residents of Canada must correctly answer a time-related arithmetical skill-testing question. Affidavits and prizes that are refused or undeliverable will result in alternate winners randomly drawn. The First Prize winner may be asked for the use of their name and photo without additional compensation. Income tax and other taxes are prize winners' responsibility.

4) For a major prize winner list, Canadian residents send a stamped, self addressed envelope to Gold Eagle Winner Headquarters, Suite 157, 238 Davenport Road, Toronto, Ontario M5R 1J6. United States residents send a stamped, self-addressed envelope to Gold Eagle Winner Headquarters, P.O. Box 182, Bowling Green Station, New York, NY 10274. Winner list requests may not include entries and must be received by January 31, 1986 for response.

A division of
WORLDWIDE LIBRARY®

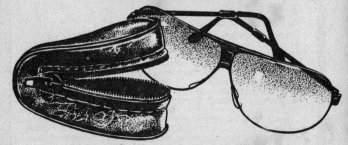